THE HEAD OF THE SAINT

THE HEAD OF THE SAINT

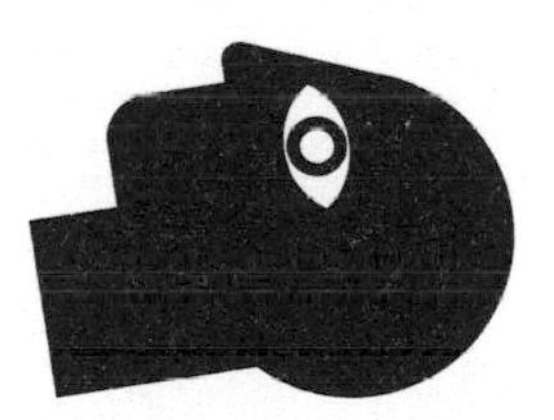

SOCORRO ACIOLI

Translation by Daniel Hahn

DELACORTE PRESS

 Published in the United States by Delacorte Press, an imprint of Random House Children's Books, a division of Penguin Random House LLC, New York.

Originally published in Portuguese as *A cabeça do santo* by Companhia das Letras, São Paulo, Brazil, in 2014. *A cabeça do santo* copyright © 2014 by Socorro Acioli. Subsequently published in English in hardcover by Hot Key Books, London, United Kingdom, in 2014. Work published with the support of the Ministry of Culture of Brazil/National Library Foundation.

Delacorte Press is a registered trademark and the colophon is a trademark of Penguin Random House LLC.

Quotes in epigraph taken with permission from:
O Vendedor de Passados by José Eduardo Agualusa (Dom Quixote, 2004)
AvóDezanove e o segredo do soviético by Ondjaki (Caminho, 2008)

Visit us on the Web! randomhouseteens.com

Educators and librarians, for a variety of teaching tools, visit us at
RHTeachersLibrarians.com

Library of Congress Cataloging-in-Publication Data
Acioli, Socorro.
[A cabeça do santo. English]
The head of the saint / Socorro Acioli ; translated by Daniel Hahn. —
First American edition.
pages cm
"Originally published in Portuguese by Companhia das Letras, São Paulo, Brazil in 2014. Originally published in English in hardcover by Hot Key Books, London, United Kingdom in 2014. Work published with the support of the Ministry of Culture of Brazil/National Library Foundation."
Summary: Having arrived in Candeia, Brazil, starving and footsore, after walking sixteen days to fulfill his dying mother's last wishes, young Samuel takes up residence in an enormous, broken statue of Saint Anthony and finds that he can hear the prayers of the townspeople, despite his lack of faith.
ISBN 978-0-553-53792-5 (hc) — ISBN 978-0-553-53794-9 (glb) —
ISBN 978-0-553-53793-2 (ebook) [1. Homeless persons—Fiction. 2. Faith—Fiction. 3. Prayer—Fiction. 4. Fathers and sons—Fiction. 5. Supernatural—Fiction. 6. Anthony, of Padua, Saint, 1195–1231—Fiction.] I. Hahn, Daniel, translator.
II. Title.
PZ7.1.A22He 2016
[Fic]—dc23
2014048063

The text of this book is set in 10.8-point Charter ITC.
Interior design by Stephanie Moss

Printed in the United States of America
10 9 8 7 6 5 4 3 2 1
First American Edition

For Gabriel García Márquez,

Maria Julia Tadeo

and Alquimia Peña,

for that December that changed everything

If you knew the things I believe in, you'd look at me as though I were a whole great circus of monsters.

—José Eduardo Agualusa, *O Vendedor de Passados*

"Stories from way back then, are they the ones that have come from a long time ago?"
"Yes, my boy."
"So way back then is a time, then, Grandma?"
"Way back then is a place."
"Quite a faraway place?"
"Quite an inside place."

—Ondjaki, *AvóDezanove e o segredo do soviético*

PART ONE

CHARITY

He was no longer wearing shoes, and his feet, by now, had turned into something else: a pair of deformed animals. Two filthy, toothy things. Two wild creatures attached to his ankles, untiring, moving forward, one after another, leading Samuel on for sixteen long, painful days under the sun.

For the first of those days, blood and water seeped from the burst blisters on his feet and hissed as they touched the harsh, red-hot tarmac. Now his feet were dry, so dry they made no sound at all. A new layer of skin had appeared, almost a snakeskin—a shriveled thing, an impressive achievement from nature. His legs were a paradox: the thinner they got, the stronger they became. His muscles grew, even on the dirty shins that supported his emaciated thighs. And his body, as dirty as if newly exhumed, walked constantly straight ahead.

Sixteen days. Sometimes he would look down, afraid that

his belly would be clinging to his ribs. Like in the story of the fallen man that his mother, Mariinha, used to tell him. That day, she would say, had been very hot—with more than just the hot wind they were used to. She had heard the sound of someone outside, clapping to attract her attention. She went to open the door, ready with the modest happiness that she always shared with her neighbors or those who bought hats from her. Her smile disappeared with the shock of what she found: a man lying on the floor, so starved that the skin over his stomach clung to his ribs. The man was handsome, and it was this that saved him. The women in the neighborhood lost no time in boiling him up a cornmeal porridge, roasting a fat chicken, making a kilo of sautéed rice with garlic and salt, frying a large pan of manioc flour mixed with dried beef and coriander, pouring nine glasses of milk with cinnamon and boiling eight eggs. There was no shortage of volunteers to deliver the dishes, to feed him, shave him, clean his face with a piece of cloth scented with cologne. It took two days of the unfortunate man gorging on food for his belly to unstick from his ribs with a loud, dry popping sound that could be heard right across Horto. He returned from the land of the dead with such desire that it took him no time at all to ask for the hand of one of the girls in marriage. The girl was Estelita, the one who had brought him the cornmeal porridge.

Samuel's own belly was almost stuck to his ribs, too, and he could only hope it would still be possible to unstick it when the time came. Would anybody help him? Would anyone bring food to a walking dead man? He thought about roast chicken, about bananas, about his mother's hands filling his milky-white porcelain plate, with its chipped edges and little peeling floral design. His mother's hands were something he tried not to remember. The memory was a pain that had no name.

Shoes, trouser legs, shirtsleeves, just a little money: everything had been left behind along the way. (Amazing, but there are people who will buy shirtsleeves.) His ill-protected torso was two different colors. His arms, sunburned now, were no use for anything but to support his hands. Of all the things a body requires, he had almost none of them. His body beseeched and punished him in equal measure. The suitcase he had been carrying when he set off from home was traded on the fifth day. It was that or starvation. He swapped it for a dish of cooked meat and bean stew. The owner of a boardinghouse had agreed, reluctantly, only because she needed a suitcase to keep her tablecloths in.

All he had left were the few words of the address in his left-hand pocket. In the heat he worried that the little piece of paper would roast and the only clue to his destiny would catch fire. Samuel would put his hand in his pocket desperately: that would be the worst of the day's whole roster of nightmares. He wanted to get there, to the place described in those eight words and one number. Getting there was the only purpose he had in life.

His smooth dark hair had grown quickly and was already flopping irritatingly over his forehead, obstructing his vision. He had small eyes, generous eyebrows that met above his nose, a fleshy mouth and other features that he had inherited from his mother.

Samuel's was a thin, hungry body, almost a shadow,

which didn't stop walking. Almost ten hours of walking a day. Not much water, scant food, sleep only in brief bursts. He shed everything along the way: youth, happiness, bits of skin, milliliters of sweat, kilos of flesh and the paltry remaining threads of faith that there might be something invisible on earth that could help men. This faith had never been his own—it was Mariinha's; he would borrow it only seldom. At that moment, Samuel didn't have the slightest faith in matters of the spirit.

On the other side of the road, meanwhile, walking toward the place he'd come from, were perfect examples of his extreme opposite.

CANDEIA

They were eight people of faith: three men, two women, three children. All of them in exactly the same tunic of thick brown fabric that St. Francis used to wear, so they believed. A cord tied round the waist, a few provisions. Not a lot: they were at the end of their journey, wilted and empty. They walked away from the towering statue of St. Francis of Canindé, brown and huge, with its palms outstretched.

They were walking slowly, the younger man on his knees, the others close around him. The smaller children were being carried; the older one was on foot and endured his penance without complaint, not realizing he did not yet owe any saint anything at all. They babbled the whole time, praying constantly, for the saint was listening to them. They walked under the gaze of St. Francis so that he might see them, see their sacrifice, and look kindly upon the petitions they brought with them.

It didn't take long for them to notice the lone half-naked youth on the other side of the road. One of the women hurriedly took a bottle of water out of her cloth bag, as well as a rag, a flask of rubbing alcohol, a bit of dry bread. They were there to help him, just as St. Francis helped them. She and her husband ran over to take care of this presumed pilgrim boy. The closer they got, the more painfully apparent his wretched condition was.

"You won't lack for charity, brother. St. Francis is watching you!" said the woman, quick and devoted.

Samuel took the bottle and drank the water desperately, letting it run down the sides of his mouth, his neck, his chest.

"St. Francis will give you strength, brother! You will find solace in his blessings," said her husband with a smile.

"But I'm not a pilgrim, *senhor,*" said Samuel, his rotten breath laced with sarcasm. "I just want to know whether it's still far to Candeia, but if you do have more food, I'd also be grateful for that."

The woman was enraged. He wasn't a pilgrim; he was some good-for-nothing kid—a thief, a rapist, a murderer, a swindler. . . . No good at all, that was for sure. A good kid doesn't walk filthy along the road or respond in that way to the charity of those trying to lessen his afflictions. Her analysis of his character had moved, in mere moments, from one end of the scale to the other. She threw the dry bread onto the ground and crossed the road back to her people. Her husband remained; he knew a bit more about life and having patience for human weakness. He had already seen a lot of decent people going crazy on the Chagas road—it was a regular occurrence. In all these years as a pilgrim he had seen everything on the road and had learned to take pity, because sometimes God does deliver man from his madness. The Devil is an artist. Few are they who can escape Satan's tricks.

He pointed over to the statue of St. Francis and showed Samuel how close he already was to reaching the foot of the saint.

"Candeia is on the slopes of St. Francis, on this side of the road, after Canindé. Go with God, brother."

Samuel didn't answer. The pilgrim smiled, just slightly. His eyes were trying to express faith and strength to the weakened youth.

Samuel felt much stronger having met the man and drunk the water. The man watched him from the other side of the road as Samuel quickened his pace and saw that he really was close to Candeia. In this the pilgrim had been useful, he thought. He could already spot a few houses out in the distance, to the right. He looked at the piece of paper in his pocket: "Niceia Rocha Vale, Manoel Vale, Rua da Matriz, 52."

CAFÉ

Candeia had almost nothing to it. A collection of dead houses, a little old church, the remnants of a square. Some of the buildings didn't even have a roof, and others had been taken over by the forest and were missing their walls. Even the windless air seemed to have lost all hope. It was hard to believe that anyone lived here.

The only sign of life came from an open café. Two wooden tables were out front, and beside those a truck, with a man and a woman in the driver's cab. They listened to music, hugged and kissed each other. It was even more sad and desolate than Horto Hill, this village—much more. In Horto, part of Juazeiro do Norte, there were people, the town was alive. And in the midst of all those people it was always possible to find a good soul, like his mother, a pretty girl, a lively friend. Candeia was dead. It was especially bad at this time of day, when even the sun was ending its life.

Samuel was a little glad, though, to hear the truck driver's music. He almost smiled. This quick wisp of gladness lasted until the appearance of a terrifying woman through the badly painted blue café door. She was cursing, with a broom in her hand, and shouting to the truck driver to turn that bloody music off. The driver addressed her by name.

"Where's my coffee, Helenice? Stop grumbling, you old terror!"

Out of the same door now appeared a young woman, very young, with a red thermos and two cups. She came and went quickly, bringing two plates, four small bread rolls, two baked bananas and a tub of margarine.

"Five *reais,*" commanded Helenice, her hand on the thermos. "If you don't pay, you don't eat."

Laughing at Helenice the whole time, the man paid. He was visibly drunk, constantly trying to bite the woman in the driver's cab, who was badly dressed, wretched, half-naked, pretty ugly. It seemed almost impossible that all this should be contained within a single person.

Samuel envied the driver and the food that he ate. He remembered Mariinha, who liked tapioca pancakes with coffee. That was how they were, these memories of Mariinha, always surfacing, wordless; photos from a memory, hurried scenes. With a scent, sometimes. Always her scent.

Helenice took her broom back inside, and the girl went round to the side of the house. Samuel followed her, giving no thought to how much more frightening his presence would be in the twilight.

"Please, for the love of God, can you spare any bread?"

He didn't recognize himself in this boy who used God's name to ask for bread, but he had learned on Horto Hill that the only way to move people in this lost part of the world was to threaten that God was watching everything and that He would not forgive a lack of charity.

The girl jumped at the sound of his voice. He saw a mixture of fear and pity in her face as she said a hurried "Wait there" and came back quickly, tossing him a bag.

His hunger didn't stop him from noticing how attractive the girl was, with a fine body and honey eyes. Samuel reached into the bag and attacked the old bread fiercely, gnawing desperately at it and choking on the dry crusts. His face quickly turned purple, he couldn't breathe—he'd always eaten too fast since he was a kid. It wasn't a pretty sight.

The girl took a bottle that was dirty with something and filled it with water from the tap. She handed it to the suffocating boy, who drank—all flustered—and cleared his throat. She felt sorry for him. Perhaps he was even her age. It would have been better if he had been old, really old—that way he would be harmless and she could help him more. Maybe then even her mother would take pity on him, too. The girl had a selfish thought: he was suffering more than she was. How good it was to see someone suffering more. How good. That wretched destiny, however it might have come about, made her own fate a little lighter. She had never thought she would find someone who suffered more than she did. But she had, just for a moment.

Helenice appeared in a rage and shooed Samuel out with her broom, as though he were an animal. She was the animal, not him, Samuel thought, still coughing. She asked the girl to take the bottle from him, but the girl didn't do what she was told. She ran into the café while Helenice launched herself at Samuel, yelling, brandishing the broom as though it were a sword. There was nothing for him to do but run.

He was in Candeia, at last, but where nobody knew him. Where he had only just arrived and already been chased off with a broomstick, where he'd only managed to get a bag of dry bread with dirty water, where it was hard to believe anyone lived, where the sun was beginning to take its leave.

Three potbellied little boys, practically naked, were running through those Saturday afternoon streets. The dust, the thin cats, everything suffered from desolation and despair.

He sat down on a bit of pavement to continue eating the dry crusts, more carefully this time. He drank some water, slowly, until he saw a tap on the wall of the house next to where he was sitting. Now he drank as much as he wanted; he'd be able to refill the bottle, even wash his face before seeking out the address. He was there to find a house, find a woman, ask after a man, settle an ancient debt and then leave. It should not take long. He was driven more by fury than planning. He trusted he'd know what to do when the time came.

He used the tap to wet his hands, his face, his hair; tried to remove the black mud that was cemented under his big, hard nails. He examined himself in the mirror of an old motorbike and saw how atrocious he looked. This wasn't how he wanted to show up at the house, to talk to Niceia. But this wasn't how he had imagined his own life—and yet here he was, transformed into the son of the Devil, in this town where no one knew him.

It was on his journey from Juazeiro to Candeia that the Devil first appeared to Samuel. He had appeared as his father. The only father he had ever known, for he had had no father at all before that. It had been a night like any other, and he was asleep in the middle of the forest close to Inhamuns. He dreamed that Mariinha, who was dressed as a bride, was smiling at someone, and that she walked over to a man and that man was a monster, the Devil. The Devil looked like Samuel, in a way, while being simultaneously monstrous. It was the only image Samuel had of his father: the picture of a Ferocious Beast.

Samuel remembered this as he felt the water running low out of the tap, losing strength to just a thread. Even the water seemed to be dying.

The owner of the house—and of the tap—was walking slowly up the pavement. She was arm in arm with a decrepit old man, who stared hard as though he could no longer move his eyes. He was like the smoke left at the end of a bonfire. On the pavement, two chairs were comfortably covered with faded floral-pattern cushions. First the woman settled the old man in a chair, talked to him, smiled, showed him this and that, as though unaware of his frailness. She called a yellow cat by name, Jerimum, and he responded by jumping onto the man's lap. Perhaps it was an old habit—cats are given to routine—but the old man didn't seem to notice his presence. Were they friends once? Samuel wondered. Could it be that the cat was also an ancient thing close to death?

Samuel stood watching it all from the pavement, until the old woman spotted him when she was already settled in her chair. Even his dreadful appearance was not enough to frighten her, and her kindness matched exactly the description Mariinha had given of his grandmother, Niceia—a good-hearted woman. As she sat holding hands with the unresponsive old man, she smiled and said hello to Samuel. Without knowing exactly what he was saying—being smiled at had confused him more than being driven off with a broom—Samuel took the piece of paper from his pocket and asked whether she was Niceia. No, her name was Rosa. Then he asked where the Rua da Matriz was.

"It's that one. It goes right by the Matriz church."

They were right next to the road. She was still smiling.

"And the house of Niceia Rocha Vale?"

The old man mumbled something, a distressing noise—guttural, almost desperate.

"He wants water," she translated for Samuel.

Still holding the old man's hand, she stood up and called to someone over the wall. No one came. She went into the house to fetch some water, helped the old man drink, calmed him down and helped him to his feet, steadying his legs and supporting his frail body—then the two of them went in, the woman giving a quick goodbye wave without looking at Samuel or answering his question. Samuel was sure that the old man had been trying to reply.

CLOUDS

He hadn't been in Candeia an hour and Samuel was already on the Rua da Matriz, following the old lady's directions. It was all too quick. He'd thought it would take him longer before he—well, before he was face to face with his grandmother and his father. What would he say? He didn't think about it, but he remembered Mariinha's voice, word for word, asking him to go and find them.

If he could do it, he would kill his father. He had never killed before, and he had no weapon and no idea how big the man was. But he was motivated by the years of history, by the last fortnight especially: Mariinha's face, her quiet little voice, her four requests. He took a deep breath and off he went.

It didn't take Samuel long to find the house. It was the biggest on the street, close to the church. Everything was still dead. Before calling out from the gate for someone, he looked around. The doors and windows on the street were bricked up. Weeds grew up over the tiles, coming out through the gaps, roots breaking through the floor of the pavements and verandas, overwhelming the stone. The houses were built around the square. On many of them it was still possible to read words written in old, peeling paint. "St. Anthony Barber," "St. Anthony's," "St Anthony Hostel," "St. Anthony Restaurant." Faded traces of a past he didn't understand. Why was everything so abandoned, so desperate?

Once again his feet were overtaken by a sudden burst of courage. It was the Ferocious Beast, he believed that. His father, the Devil. The life he had led over the past few days had made it seem more possible to believe in evil. He took the piece of paper out of his pocket—he had to read them one more time, those eight words and the number that were already embedded in his memory, and do what had to be done here. Then he could leave.

He clapped his hands and leaned against the iron gate, which was chained and padlocked. There was a garden in front, overgrown by the forest. Overgrown by the forest and overrun by the cats. Eight or nine of them, with more and more appearing. It was a big house, with a porch and a rusty rocking chair. There was a grille in front of the wooden door, and it only took two claps for the inner door to open and an indescribable woman to come out.

"Are you Dona Niceia?"

"And you're Samuel."

It was not a question. It was not a smile. It was not a welcome.

"Do you know me?"

"No. Nor do you know yourself. But I know who you are."

She looked crazy, and her words sounded crazy, too.

"Are you hungry?" asked the old woman.

"Very."

"I can tell by looking at you."

". . ."

"Have you come from Juazeiro?"

"Yes."

"And you haven't brought me anything?"

"No."

"Your mother told you to."

"She did, but I didn't bring it."

"How did you get here?"

"I walked."

"The whole way?"

"Yes."

"How many days?"

"A couple of weeks."

"Sixteen days."

"How do you know?"

"I know."

"And Manoel?"

"Which Manoel?"

"Your son."

"Oh yes—my Manoel . . ." A cloud of tears drifted across her face, and she looked down, showing her scalp through her thin white hair.

"Does he live here in town?"

"This is no longer a town."

"Where does he live?"

"That's one of God's mysteries. He has many."

"Did he move away from here a long time ago?"

There was no answer. She looked at Samuel.

"So he lives here?"

"There's no point trying to get in." She held the door with both hands. Her expression had changed—she was angry now.

"Is he alive?"

"You said you were hungry?"

"Very."

The change of subject worked.

"And dirty. You need a bath."

Samuel was sure she was going to invite him in, and then, perhaps later or the next day, he could ask for details about what had happened to Manoel, his father. If he was already dead, it would save Samuel his trouble. Perhaps he would stay there awhile—the idea of a house to sleep in was just what he needed after sixteen days of sleeping rough like a dog in the road. If she had spotted that he was in need of a bath, the invitation would soon follow, he thought. But it didn't. He looked up at the house. Something told him that Manoel lived there and was hiding, maybe sensing that his son hadn't come to ask him for his blessing.

Niceia spoke again: "It's already dark, and it'll be raining soon. Leave here now, and follow this road. Go past the Matriz church and the cemetery, go into the forest itself, straight ahead. Don't turn off anywhere. When you spot a guava tree, take the path off to the right. There's a covered spot there where you can rest. Run now, and get some sleep. There's a big storm coming."

She slammed the old wooden door and disappeared. There was no trace of any sound coming from inside. This whole time, Samuel had been pressed up against the iron gate, the woman with disheveled hair on the other side. This wasn't how Mariinha had described old Niceia. This wasn't how he had imagined meeting his grandmother.

Had she summoned the rain, called it to come? Just moments earlier, the sky had been clear, with no sign that the clouds were about to shed their tears. Now all the clouds in the sky cried at once.

CANINES

The first person in Samuel's family to know the date of her own death was his great-great-grandmother Mafalda. She put in her earrings, put on perfume and lipstick, put on her Sunday clothes at bedtime and went to say goodbye to her daughter.

"Look, Toinha, this is my last day. My mother said she and Aunt Amália are coming to fetch me. The livestock belongs to you and your brother, divided up. If you sell it, divide it up; if you kill it, divide it up. The house is yours, as your brother's already got his own. And what's here is yours. Table, chair, bed, water filter, jug—everything."

Her daughter was in the kitchen picking through the beans and laughed without even looking up, because that was senile old woman's talk. Mafalda was healthy and showed no sign of death.

Again Mafalda informed her that she would be going and

not coming back. Which is what she did. She never awoke again, dead and cold. In her Sunday dress, earrings and lipstick. Her daughter cried twice for her mother's death: once for losing her and once for not having taken the opportunity to say goodbye. She had so much to say, and the words that were not said to the dead woman would burn in her mouth forever.

That was how it happened with all the women in the family, and with Mariinha it was no different. They all knew the exact number of days that would make up the collection of hours that we call life. They knew it from early on and kept it to themselves, but announced it in time to make requests of their families and make arrangements. Mariinha called Samuel to her and told him that Thursday would be her last day.

They lived in a shabby little house on the slopes of Horto Hill, on the path that led to the white statue of Father Cicero. But she wasn't from around there. She had come to Juazeiro when she found herself alone with a child in her arms. Since the boy was going to be raised with no father, he might as well at least be the godson of Padim—Father Cicero—blessed by him day and night. Mariinha fell into the graces of Glória—Glória the blessed—who took care of her like a daughter. She soon learned how to weave straw and sell hats to the pilgrims. And that was how she lived and raised her son for fifteen years. Samuel's father had left Tauá when Mariinha was pregnant. His mother had told him to return to Candeia for some important work. She didn't give any details, and it was expensive to telephone. He was going to earn some money, Manoel told Mariinha, then he would come back for her and Samuel and they would live together in a house with a veranda, the best in Candeia.

Mariinha always knew it would be a boy. She was wise, it was as simple as that; she didn't need to take exams to prove it. She chose what she thought was the most beautiful name in the world, something she'd learned at Mass. Manoel liked it, and talked to her stomach, calling his son by his name and promising to come back. It would only be for six months or so, he said. "I'll be back soon, Mariinha." Never. He never came back. In the first month he sent a carrier with money and a letter with his mother's address. It was just when Mariinha's belly had started to show. Mariinha left Tauá and went to Juazeiro. She had only a father and an older sister, who didn't want a fallen woman in their house. She left messages with everyone in town to say where she was going. So that he could find them. But there was nothing, no news from Manoel ever again.

Mariinha waited her whole life, every day. Samuel waited beside her, until he was six years old and his school friends told him his mother was a tramp. A single mother and a prostitute were the same thing. The shadow of his father was the boy's unhappiness for years.

"I'm going on Thursday, Samuel. My mother has said she's coming to fetch me."

It wasn't an announcement of a short trip. To Mariinha, going meant going away forever. Samuel didn't really believe in these stories of deaths foretold to the women of his family. He had never known any of them; he had only heard about these announcements but never seen them fulfilled. If it was true, he would have no one left in this world. His mother had little life in her eyes now, little flesh on her bones. She said she had four things to ask him before going, and Samuel sensed that they would not be easy things to hear.

"I want you to light three candles for my soul. The first in the sanctuary of my own Father Cicero, the second at the statue of St. Francis of Canindé, on whatever day you're able to get there, no need to hurry. And the third is to St. Anthony, because he is my mother's patron saint. All three at their feet, my child, right by their feet, that's important to me. But my greater wish is that you go to Candeia to seek out your grandmother and your father." She took an old piece of paper out of a cloth bag. The eight words and the number. "Her name, your grandmother's, is Niceia. She ought to know where your father is. Go without hate. Dona Niceia is a good woman, and you have no one else in the world now. She came to see me once, she came to meet you. If she never came back, it's because she couldn't. I want you to take my Mother of God rosary to her."

Samuel tried, but he couldn't hide his hatred. He could see no reason for seeking out those people who had never taken the least interest in his existence. The man must have another family now and surely wouldn't even remember him.

"I know you want nothing to do with this, but it's the last thing I'm asking of you. My soul will never be at peace if you don't do it. Look for him; God will help you. Will you go, Samuel? Will you go to look for your father?"

Samuel said yes to the four requests: the candle for Father Cicero, another candle for St. Francis, one more for St. Anthony, and the search for his grandmother and father.

And it happened just as she had said it would. She slowly died, a bit of life escaping from her each day. On Thursday night, Mariinha no longer moved her eyes. She turned cold, bit by bit, and then she was dead, no coming back.

There were lots of people to bear the tattered old hammock holding the thin body of the good woman, Mariinha from Horto, known to everyone in Juazeiro do Norte. So many years spent making hats, patiently weaving. Anyone who wanted to know how to do it learned from her. Any hat bought in Horto had Mariinha's goodness deep in the weft of woven yellow straw. The mourners, all of them, cried from genuine grief. Not even they, professional mourners who saw the deceased daily, could get used to her death.

Samuel packed the old leather suitcase that same day and set off on Saturday. The same suitcase that Mariinha had carried from Tauá to Juazeiro. He left the few things in the house to his good neighbors, women who cried for the death of his mother and the departure of her son, so embittered, so sad.

He left for Candeia. Not out of obedience, but because there had been no time to say he wouldn't go. Mariinha had died believing it.

Night fell and he followed Niceia's instructions, because it did indeed start raining and there was nothing to be done but seek some shelter. He couldn't tell whether his grandmother's so-called goodness was his mother's innocent lie or one of Mariinha's mistakes from being unable to see badness anywhere. The old woman hadn't even opened the door for him. No glass of water, plate of food, place to sleep . . . nothing.

He went on into the forest, picking up his pace because of the rain. He spotted the dry guava tree. Five thin wild dogs came running down the little hill right in front of him, barking. The smallest, a white dog with a star-shaped black marking on its forehead, attacked his shin, sinking its teeth in mercilessly. Samuel cried out to nobody as the dogs continued barking loudly. Then a distant whistling sound made the animals prick up their ears and they shot off, up the same path on which they'd come, to somewhere that was too dark to see. Were it not for the bleeding bite on his leg, Samuel would have thought them ghost dogs.

Struggling to walk, blood streaming from his leg, he found the entrance to a foul, dark cave. The old woman had spoken of a covered nook to sleep in, and this had to be it. It was raining even more heavily now, and there was no trace of light left. Samuel crawled into the filthy grotto and sat down with his leg sticking out, to wash the blood from the bite, which was burning. The rainwater had soaked his bread, and all he had now was a white slime for his dinner. He could hear the faint, sharp, hysterical shrieks of the rats as they ran out. Overwhelmed with tiredness he fell asleep, despite the rats, the pain, and the hunger. Good or bad, it was his first night-long sleep in many days.

CAVE

It was exactly five in the morning when Samuel began to wake, tormented and confused. He could hear women's voices, several of them, all talking at once. Talking, talking, talking. It was like a prayer, an argument, a conversation, all at once. Perhaps it was a nightmare. They sounded like Mariinha's mourner friends, praying the rosary when people died. He sat up, startled, but the voices didn't stop. Louder, stronger, and—yes—it was prayer. Samuel ran out of the damned grotto without remembering that his leg was injured, that he was weak, hungry and tired, and within a few feet he'd fallen to the ground. There were no women praying outside at all; there was no one nearby, not even last night's dogs. Outside there was only forest, a fine rain and silence: no voices to be heard.

When he turned to look at where he was, with the help of the scarce light from the overcast sun, Samuel saw that the grotto was in fact a giant head, hollow and startling. The head of a saint. Although overgrown with plants, it was possible to see how grotesque the nose was—two huge holes—the face turned up toward the sky, with thick, closed lips, bulging eyes, a serious expression. The eyeballs were the most frightening part: a couple of concrete balls attached by steel cables to the hollow eyes. The head was made up of symmetrical pieces that had been numbered in white paint and fitted together. Samuel struggled to his feet and walked closer.

It was a hallucination, he thought. A bite from a mad dog and he'd gone crazy, too. Yet the day was getting lighter and Samuel could clearly see the strange grotto, big enough for him to stand up in. The neck to the crown of the head was almost the size of the little house where he had lived with Mariinha. Yes, it really was the head of a saint—hollow, huge, terrifying and forest-covered. A decapitated saint was his only shelter in the world. It was with that thought that he went back inside.

The wound to his leg was hurting more and more, and the skin around it became gradually hotter. He wasn't sure he could walk now. There was a little water left in the bottle and only a bit of soft bread. From inside the head he spotted the guava tree again and saw its low-hanging green fruits. He thought that he might be able to make it over there, and he shuffled along, wincing with each step. He saw the head again—terrifying—but this time he also looked up to the top of the hill. He blinked in amazement when he realized the rest of the saint's body was standing up there.

Perhaps some giant had decapitated the saint, he thought. He'd slashed through his neck with a sword and the head had rolled down the hill. There was no other way to explain that aberration: the head had rolled down like a ball and come to rest here. Gray, unpainted. Not the white of Father Cicero, not the colors of St. Francis. Samuel laughed to himself, laughed at the decapitated saint, picked green guavas from the tree and limped back into the head. He laughed out of fear.

He bit into the worm-eaten fruit, swallowed the caterpillars, appeased his hunger. It rained the whole day, and that was good. Samuel sat outside the head and took off his clothes to wash himself. He discovered that by the side of the saint's eye a spout formed that was just right for filling the bottle so he could drink the rainwater. The tears of the saint, Mariinha would have said. He spent the day like this, bearing the pain, remembering his mother, washing his wound, drinking rainwater.

When it was evening he fell asleep again, waking on the dot of five in the morning with the same women's voices tormenting what was left of his common sense. Again: when he looked there was nobody outside. Samuel pressed his ear to the concrete and managed to hear one of the voices more clearly. It was a prayer, very clear: a petition to St. Anthony.

The fact was that the women's prayers were reverberating inside the head of the saint and, for some reason, Samuel could hear them. The following day he ate guavas and leaves, drank rainwater, and noticed that the prayers were being made in the morning and in the evening, too. Not always all the voices, not always all the same words, but the one thing that remained constant was their petition: they were in love or they wanted to marry.

Samuel spent four days inside the head, eating guavas and leaves from the surrounding trees, drinking rainwater. The wound had gotten much worse. Hunger and fever were making him sicker every day, unable even to stand now. He would have been condemned to die inside that extraordinary tomb were it not for the blow to his back that he received on the fourth day.

A package fell in through the saint's nose, bouncing off Samuel's back where he lay. He twisted round to see several plastic bags with something inside them falling into the head. When Samuel tried to drag himself over to reach the parcels, a kid crawled into the grotto, immediately grabbed a package, and, shining a torch on it, opened it. After unwrapping lots and lots of bags, he pointed the weak torchlight onto the pages he was holding in one of his hands. They were pornographic magazines.

"What the hell is all this?"

The boy gave a loud yell at the shock. His only reflex was to yank his trousers up quickly, pale and terrified.

Samuel laughed out everything that he had kept inside him in all those recent serious days. He roared with laughter at how pathetic it was, this sight of a kid reading porn mags inside the head of a decapitated saint. He'd seen a lot in Juazeiro, but this was really too much.

His name was Francisco, the boy told Samuel, and he was thirteen. He had discovered the hiding place a year earlier, more or less, and had been going in secret ever since. He got the magazines from the truck driver who stopped at the Candeia café, and the head of the saint was the only safe place to go with them.

Unsteadily, Francisco stood up to leave, clearly still astonished by the discovery of Samuel in the saint's head.

"If you get me some food," said Samuel, "I won't tell anyone about your bad behavior."

"What are you, a bandit?"

"Not yet, but I do want to kill people I hate."

"Are you running away from the police?"

"Not yet."

"What are you doing here?"

"I've come to find my Devil of a father, but as soon as I have I'll be leaving right away. I'm only in here because of this wound to my leg. I won't be living in your castle, you needn't worry about that."

The boy looked at the wound with an expression of disgust. It was filled with pus, swollen and purple.

"Is there a hospital here?" Samuel asked.

"No, just a health center."

"And is there a doctor?"

"Only Fridays."

"What day is today?"

"Saturday."

Samuel thought for a moment.

"Francisco, if you can take me to the health center on

Friday, I'll get some medicine. Then I can leave your head in peace. Both heads."

"When did you get here?"

"A few days ago."

"And what have you been living on?"

"Green guava. But I've eaten some leaves, too."

"What medicine do you need to put on that leg?"

"Who knows? Rubbing alcohol?"

"It'll sting like hell."

"Do you know somewhere to get any?"

"At home we've got ointment for cuts. I'll bring some."

"If you want to bring a bit of food, I'll eat anything. I'm scared I'll die in here."

"That's all we need, a dead body appearing inside the head of the saint. That's sure to make anyone who's still left in this place go completely nuts."

"The more you help me, the quicker I'll get out of here. And I won't tell anyone about your hiding place."

Francisco left. It didn't take much for him to succumb to Samuel's ridiculous blackmail.

He returned later that same day, bringing the ointment that his mother used to treat boils. He sat there awhile to chat, as if he was trying to understand. Francisco's curiosity seemed gradually to overtake his fear. He began to visit Samuel every day, bringing him food and water in secret. He didn't have any rubbing alcohol, but he did find a bottle of alcohol—cachaça—to clean the pus, so that at least the wound would not get any worse.

Going to the head of the saint every day was a huge risk

for Francisco; it would almost be a crime in the eyes of the people of Candeia, for the town had been condemned to a slow death because of that hollow skull. But to Francisco, it was better to run the risk than to be turned in. If this kid told anybody about the magazines, he was done for. Besides, the outsider's company had become good fun. Samuel liked to chat.

COAL

"Can you hear them, too?"

"What?"

"Those women, with all their praying in here."

"No one comes to pray in here. The people of Candeia hate this head."

"Why?"

"It's the curse of this town. What do you mean, all their praying?"

"Since my first night here I've heard their voices asking the saint to help them find love. There's one girl who only talks about someone called Dr. Adriano. . . ."

"And who is the girl?"

"I don't know her name. Her voice comes out right here."

Samuel pointed at the exact place in the saint's head where he heard the voice come from, just above the right ear.

"I've not heard anything, not ever."

"What time is it?"

Francisco looked at his watch and paused a moment.

"Four-forty."

"It starts at five—morning and evening."

"Are you crazy?"

"Might be, who knows . . . ?"

"I think you are."

"You'll have to wait and see."

And as Francisco waited with a look of suspicion, Samuel talked a bit about his wound, the dogs, the ghost town. He said that all he wanted was to leave. He talked about Father Cicero, about the pilgrimages, about the days when he used to wake up early to sell hats on Horto Hill and how there were no hats to sell anymore. He started talking about his mother but quickly changed the subject. He said all the things he hadn't been able to say in those silent days—and then the voices began. Each one sprang from somewhere different. On the right side of the head, two handspans above the ear, came the voice of the girl who was in love with the doctor:

"My dear little saint, listen to me: I'll take you out from under my bed if Dr. Adriano marries me, I promise I'll do it right away and make a really nice altar in my house for you. Listen, dear saint, I want to go to the health center on Friday, but I don't know what excuse to give my mother; I'm not ill at all. My mother gets these ideas into her head. If she finds out I'm going to the health center, she'll close the café and come with me. I've already stolen one of his socks, my dear saint, I've already done the magic rituals, but nothing happens. Send me a sign, dear St. Anthony, send something straightaway so I can untie you, all right? Send the doctor to have lunch at the café, find some way of delaying the appointments so he doesn't leave too early. Do something! In the name of the Father, the Son and the Holy Spirit, Amen!"

Samuel was holding back his laughter, both at the girl's words and at the expression on the face of Francisco, who had his ear pressed to the head, indignant: "I can't hear anything."

"Well, I can tell you: there's a girl saying she likes good little Dr. Adriano. She wants to go to his office on Friday but can't think what to tell her mother. . . ."

"You're only making that up because I said the doctor was at the health center on Fridays, liar."

"I'm not, you brat, how could I have known his name? Did you by any chance tell me his name?"

"No."

"So listen: she asked the saint for some way of deceiving her mother so she could go alone. She said otherwise her mother will close the café and go with her because she's suspicious."

"Then it's Madeinusa, the daughter of Helenice from the café. We've only got one café here."

"She's the one who gave me some dry bread, and the old lady shooed me off with her broom. Her voice sounds different, but it must be the loudspeaker effect of this Devil of a saint."

"Oh man, don't call the saint a Devil, that's a sin."

"Right, and reading a magazine with naked women inside the head of a saint is not a sin?"

"And there isn't anyone else praying, then?" Francisco changed the subject.

"Hang on."

Samuel moved himself around with a bit of trouble because of his wound. He placed the palms of his hands on the walls and slid his ear around until he could make out another voice. There were two or three more, but they were intermittent and confused.

"There's one saying, 'Forgive me, forgive me, beloved St. Anthony.'" Samuel imitated her voice.

Francisco laughed but then stopped suddenly. "No way, I'm not falling for this. You're just a bandit, you've found out about the lives of the people here and now you're trying to pull this crap with me. The head's been here all these years and no one's heard a thing. I can't hear so much as a murmur."

"But you said no one comes here, so how could you know?"

"Because lots of people from *outside* Candeia have come. At first they used the head as a toilet. Then all kinds of couples used to come—the people used to call it the Saint's Head Motel, although they stopped because they were afraid of the forest dogs. But people from the town really don't come at all."

"Damned dogs."

"Well, I don't believe a word of it. How can it be that women are praying over in their houses and the prayers end up here in the decapitated head?"

"Aren't they prayers to him?" Samuel asked.

"I suppose the prayers must travel somehow to whoever they're addressed to."

"It might be that this head makes people cleverer, because I'm getting an idea."

"Keep me out of it."

"Too late, you're already involved. There are two parts to this idea: first of all we're going to set up this girl's date with the good little doctor on Friday."

"How?"

"Hang on, I'll tell you. Listen, Francisco: between now and Friday, you keep bringing me food, water, a sheet and pillow and those magazines with naked women. If you believe in my ability to hear things, you can get your pockets ready to earn some money."

"Sounds like a whole lot of trouble."

"But if it's true, then I'm the guy who knows all the secrets of the women in this whole town. We can make money, and a lot of it."

"I don't see how. . . ."

"You know all the people in Candeia; you can tell me who's who. We'll set it all up. Arrange a wedding or wreak chaos, depending on the individual case. Blackmail brings money. I don't believe in saints, or in love. All I want is to be rich. I was born and bred selling things to pilgrims, man, trust me."

Francisco stared, deep in thought. "Are there more women talking?"

Samuel pressed his ear up against the top of the head.

"There's just one, singing, but it's quite quiet. She sings beautifully, this one. I don't even need a portable radio."

"How many are there usually?"

"Lots. But only about five or six I can hear clearly. The voices seem to be in the same places every day."

"Is she the only one who sings?"

"The only one." Samuel listened again. Nothing. "They must have stopped praying because it's time to put dinner on the table. Speaking of which, where's my food?"

Samuel stayed in the shelter till the day of the doctor's office hours, getting by with Francisco's care and studying the phenomenon of the prayers that reverberated in the huge, hollow head of St. Anthony. Samuel used a piece of coal to mark the place where each voice came through and concluded that there were only four women he could hear clearly. The others were very weak, faltering like a radio with a broken aerial. It was during this more detailed inspection of the head that Samuel spotted the letter *M,* painted in white with a circle around it. Someone had left their mark before him, but it seemed to have no connection to the voices. Just an *M,* that was all.

Francisco, who knew everybody in the town, worked out whom each of the voices belonged to. Samuel was glad he was no longer suspicious, that he had made Francisco see that there was no way he could have known so much about these women's lives, their names, the details of their routines.

The truth was, Samuel didn't understand why he was able to hear the secrets that only St. Anthony should know. Whether it was a lapse on the part of the saint, or some trick of the Devil's, there was no way of telling. It was the second-biggest event in Candeia's history. The first was the day the engineer from Rio de Janeiro told the population that the giant skull could never be lifted onto the body at the top of the hill. He was right. St. Anthony's head remained down on the ground forever. Evidence of an irreversible mistake that brought about the misfortune of the people of Candeia.

CICERO

Mariinha was twenty-five when she met Manoel, who had come to Tauá for work. She was the youngest child of the family, condemned by a backlands tradition not to marry but to take care of her father, a widower, for the rest of his life.

Manoel stayed for two months to work on a new building for the town hall. It was long enough to notice Mariinha walking past the site every day and to win her heart with flowers and letters. His wooing was full of flourishes; the bouquets he improvised had flowers from the four corners of Tauá. He spoke beautiful words, he talked of love with sweet eyes and sweet kisses, and Mariinha could not resist his advances.

The urgency of their passion bore fruit. Mariinha became pregnant near the end of Manoel's time in Tauá. Before his two months were up, though, his mother notified him of a job in his hometown of Candeia. He had no time to do his duty to Mariinha and the baby, to return to Tauá and ask Mariinha's father for her hand in marriage, to get married in church and leave everything all tidy. Except for the unsigned letter Mariinha received with his mother's address on it, Manoel disappeared. Mariinha was too proud to chase after him. Having no money, nor any certainty that he was the one who had sent the letter, there was nothing to guarantee its veracity. She didn't even know where Candeia was. Going there was not part of her plan.

It was her older sister who noticed her belly growing, her bigger breasts, her swollen nose.

"That's the belly of a pregnant woman," she said.

Their father had been eating his soup, his eyes fixed on the plate. He heard the words and continued sipping the spoonfuls noisily. Then he put the spoon down and—without raising his head—pronounced: "Tell your sister that if it is a pregnancy, she can leave this house tomorrow. I'm too old to put up with a daughter who's got a reputation."

"It is a pregnancy, Father. It's my son, Samuel."

Mariinha was able to rely on at least a shred of pity from her sister, who gave her a little money and an old leather suitcase to help her go.

She stopped at the little Tauá church before leaving, to ask forgiveness from God for her sin and pray that her son be healthy, strong and a friend to her.

The priest was in the sacristy, and Mariinha thought it would be a good idea to confess before going. She told him everything, of her sin and her passion, being thrown out by her father, the child in her belly, the loneliness she now had to face. It was this kind priest who told her that she who has faith is never alone, and suggested she go to live in the town of Juazeiro do Norte, under the eyes of Father Cicero. He gave Mariinha a blessed Mother of God rosary with blue and white beads. Mariinha noticed that there was a green bead in the place of one of the blue ones.

"Green is my lucky color," the priest explained.

He wrote on a piece of paper the names of several people he knew from when he had lived in Juazeiro. But he underlined the name of Dona Glória, the blessed, as the single most important friend to seek out.

It was said that one day Dona Glória would become a saint. She had barely turned thirteen when she was in church and a man came up to one of the side windows and gestured for her to come over. He had a message from her mother, he said. It was serious: her father had had a heart attack and he was dying. Her mother had asked this man to fetch her by bicycle because that way she would get there more quickly. Glória didn't notice anything strange about it until the bicycle was flying along a road that was nowhere near her house. When she started asking questions, sitting on the crossbar, the man told her to shut up or he'd kill her. He almost did. He raped Glória and was at the point of killing her when two men happened, miraculously, to pass by. They saved her life.

The rapist managed to get away, but he had got the poor girl pregnant. It was a public disgrace, and the town agreed that she ought to have an abortion. The doctor of Juazeiro arranged the whole thing and warned the family that the procedure carried some risk of death. That was when Glória asked her mother to call Father Cicero to give her a final blessing. To Glória's amazement, he appeared right behind her mother even before she'd finished saying his name. And he was furious. Overcome with rage.

"Get up and go and wait for your child to be born. You're quite old enough to understand what courage is. Your son will help you in life."

The father had such a presence—those black robes, those blue eyes. Glória did as she was told, running counter to everyone else, and there were many who turned their backs on her. It was a difficult birth, and she nearly died. The boy was born sick and spent his days in a hospital with Glória by his side. Nothing in their lives seemed to be as Father Cicero had predicted. They said the boy wouldn't live, that he was a testament to the sin, the memento of a crime. Only Glória, deep down, never doubted. And it was only when she was about thirty that things began to change. The boy studied, grew, became a doctor of law, went off to live in the capital and passed the examination to be a judge.

Glória never wanted to leave Juazeiro, and as the years went by her presence bore witness to a miracle. Her son, Dr. Marcelo, never set foot there again, but he sent money for the upkeep of the five-bedroom house he had bought her. Five bedrooms. She used the house to take in single mothers, and she took Mariinha in with a hug that was silent but filled with all the words the girl needed to hear. Glória looked after her in labor and taught her how to weave hats, and Mariinha looked after the older woman until the day she died. Glória the blessed.

* * *

Before leaving the town in which he had been born, Samuel walked to the statue of Father Cicero for the last time. He found it funny, this fantasy that the white statue, huge and motionless, should be able to see anything or care whether anyone lived or died in Juazeiro do Norte. His mother had believed that fantasy right up until her death.

Beside the statue there was a house for the votive offerings from those who had asked Father Cicero to bestow his graces upon them. Wooden legs and arms, bridal dresses, photographs of cars, hearts; miracles to suit every taste. Samuel lit the candle his mother had asked for with contempt for the stupid act, which as far as he was concerned had no purpose but to fill the pockets of the candle sellers—bad company whom he knew well. He watched the candle flame tremble, trying to turn into fire—that was beautiful, at least. He remembered his mother, her thin hands covered in loose, dry skin, trembling while lighting a candle. The nimble hands that had woven hats for so many years, dead now and under the earth. The hands of his mother.

He ran. He ran down Horto Hill with his suitcase in his hand. His luggage wasn't heavy, he'd never had many possessions. He walked, panting, on the road out of Juazeiro do Norte and felt a little less pain in his chest once he had left, passing over the stones that Mariinha's fragile feet would never tread again.

There was a moment on the road when he looked back and realized that he could no longer see the giant white man,

Father Cicero, who had not been strong enough to save his mother from a life of sorrows and a wretched death.

He believed that all saints were merely an invention of people who were desperate, and nothing that Mariinha had said his whole life had convinced him otherwise. Saints were stone, and only stone. That was Samuel's law.

CONVERSATION

As he recovered, Samuel's first days in Candeia were a time of some comfort compared to the wretchedness of the journey. He had a place to sleep and something to eat, by the good grace and efforts of Francisco and the blackmail about the silly secret of the porn magazines. The dogs never came back. It really did only rain on Niceia's orders, and after this one downpour the clouds seemed happy, never releasing rain again but remaining dry as cotton wool, high, like smoke in the sky. Samuel was a bit cleaner but still dressed in rags, and his hair had grown. Francisco showed him a large lake nearby where he could take a bath every now and then. It would have been ideal were the lake not the drinking place for the dogs. He saw the animals on the far bank one day and tried to leave without them spotting him. The dogs looked up at his arrival but did nothing, perhaps because it was daytime, perhaps because they only undertook to guard the hill during the night. They didn't bark when they were off duty.

The head became his house, and he set up everything more or less like a home. An old mattress with a pillow, a woolen blanket, candles, a little three-legged table, a few bottles, two glasses, a plate, cutlery—gifts from Francisco, neither bought nor stolen.

In Candeia more houses were abandoned than lived in, and after the head of the saint brought misfortune to the town, a lot of people had left without taking all of their belongings with them. The rumor that the town was cursed scared off any impressionable souls overnight.

The family in the green house, which was almost immediately facing the church, abandoned their home, leaving all their furniture: tables, sofas and beds and, on top of one of the beds, the grandmother of the family, Sara. She was the first woman to die from the curse of the head of the saint. The town only discovered her death when her cat began to meow day and night on the roof of the house. There had to be something strange going on—this cat wasn't the kind of creature to give the time of day to anyone. Dr. Adriano had gone into the abandoned house with the police chief and found poor Sara dead on the bed, her eyes open. She had died more than a week earlier, he said. She had already started to stink. Dona Sara had been married to the previous mayor—she'd been Candeia's richest woman in the good times. In the end she was buried in the family tomb by Francisco's father, the gravedigger.

It was from the green house that Francisco got the mattress, the cutlery, the pillow. It was all there because nobody went into the house. They said that it held Dona Sara's breath and that only curses could ever come out of it. They said Dona Sara still walked around the kitchen, watched television at six o'clock and said the rosary at her window on Mass day. And if someone were to go into the house, she would whisper a premonition of death. They said a lot about Sara's ghost, back when there were enough people in Candeia to spread rumors.

Francisco wasn't scared; he was the son of Chico the Gravedigger and he'd seen more dead bodies in his life than anything else. He held death in sufficiently high esteem not to be afraid of it. Every life lost was a few more coins for his father, who, besides his salary from the town hall, also earned the affection and gratitude of the families for taking care of the graves of their loved ones. Chico the Gravedigger swept the graves, washed the plastic flowers and cleaned the glass that protected the photographs on the better-off graves. The cemetery was his stone garden, his plantation of kindliness. Francisco was a regular helper. He grew up knowing that even death was something you could miss when it took its time coming.

They chatted a lot, Francisco and Samuel. They told each other the stories of their lives, from up on Horto Hill to down in the grave pits. Bit by bit they began to confide in each other. They tried to understand how it was that the prayers of the women came to be trapped within the concrete of the decapitated saint—but it was impossible. They went carefully over their plans, plotting to earn money by exploiting the carelessness of the saint who had allowed Samuel access to the prayers of his followers. They were going to make a serious impact in Candeia. They laughed at their own misfortunes and at other people's. Misfortunes were all there to be laughed at.

CONSULTATION

Thursday, five a.m. precisely. Samuel awoke with a start in his saint's-head house and pressed his ear to the mark for the voice they'd worked out to be Madeinusa's. It was on the right, just above the ear. Francisco tried, too; he had stayed over especially, as this business of the saint preferring Samuel really annoyed him. It was no use, though—he still couldn't hear anything.

Madeinusa was asking the saint to give her the strength and courage to go to see Dr. Adriano. She asked the wedding maker, St. Anthony, to find some way to make sure her mother would not suspect anything, she said amen and that was that. The plan was to say she was going to a friend's house to collect some money she was owed, because she knew that the girl had won something on the lottery in Fortaleza. Helenice was money-mad, so the plan was perfect.

Samuel and Francisco ran out without having to say a

word—their plan was all ready, too. Francisco would go to the health center, and Samuel would go and talk to Madeinusa.

And so it was.

Samuel surprised the girl in the middle of the street as she hurried along, and he walked beside her at the same pace. She was afraid.

"Listen, Madeinusa. You know I live in St. Anthony's head? He's sent you a message."

"Ha, that's all I need."

"He said he can't bear being tied up under your bed any longer."

Madeinusa went pale. This was ridiculous. How could he possibly know?

"St. Anthony said he wants to see you married to Dr. Adriano, and he has instructions for you."

"What kind of joke is this?"

"Look, you just have to go into his office and say you've got a pain in the heart. Just say that. And take the sock."

"What?"

"The doctor's sock. Take the sock with you to the appointment."

No one knew about the saint under the bed, about her passion for the doctor, the appointment and the sock—oh God! If this crazy beggar boy was talking about it, his story deserved her attention. She prayed to the saint in secret, she had stolen the sock in secret, and now this boy was revealing it all like this—it had to be for some good reason.

"Pain in the heart? What pain in the heart?"

"Don't ask me. It's a message from the saint."

Moments before the crazy boy had appeared, Madeinusa

had been wondering what she could say when she walked into the office, since she wasn't in any pain apart from the passion that was consuming her life. It made her believe the boy's words were true. All this happened so fast—the two of them spoke so quickly—that there was no time for her to think.

The next day Francisco arrived early at the health center so he could be first in the queue. Madeinusa took a little longer, and there were about eight people ahead of her. She stood at the back of the queue in a state of visible anxiety. She was pretty, Madeinusa, she always had been. Her father said that something as lovely as her must have been imported, like the radio he'd bought. The box bore the words: "Made in USA." "My daughter's name comes from abroad. All I did was put the letters together."

She wore her hair long, always tied back, her skirt below the knee, clothes buttoned up to her neck. She instinctively knew that untying her hair, rolling down the waistband of her skirt just a bit and opening one pathetic button on her blouse would make her even more beautiful, with many, many more years to live.

Samuel took his place at the front of the queue alongside Francisco. The doctor arrived right away, said good morning without looking at anyone and went into the building. He didn't even see Madeinusa as she practically fainted. She loved that man, everything she saw of him and everything she imagined he had within him.

The queue was kept in order by a health assistant, whose

job it was to note who arrived after whom and to open the office door. Her portly bearing and permanent expression of disgust averted any possibility of confusion in the order of arrivals. There was no need, there were never many people—eight, ten, fifteen of the area's residents. People came here from outside Candeia, because they knew there was almost nobody living here in need of a doctor.

She opened the door, making an abrupt gesture as if to say, "Well, go in then, idiots. . . ."

Francisco and Samuel went in. That was the deal. If Francisco took Samuel to the doctor to cure the wound on his leg and help Madeinusa, he would have the privacy of the hollow head restored to him. Samuel could leave once his leg had healed, and he could set about finding his father once more. The doctor, jotting something down, asked what the problem was. Dr. Adriano looked at the wound from a distance, not disguising his shock. It was serious.

"How did that happen?"

"A dog bite, at the saint's head."

The doctor looked up and gave Samuel a ferocious look of reproach. The boy guessed why—he had mentioned the saint's head that had condemned Candeia to wretchedness. He knew from Francisco that talking about St. Anthony was forbidden.

"I live in the head and I listen to what the saint is thinking, Doctor."

"He's trying to help the town," Francisco joined in.

"How long have you been hearing voices?"

"Since I arrived in Candeia."

"Is there any history of mental illness in your family?"

"You think I'm crazy, Doctor? I'm completely normal!"

Dr. Adriano laughed quietly to himself, because he'd learned from his psychiatry professor that crazy people always say they're sane. The prescription he wrote out was more illegible than his usual scrawl; he wanted to get rid of the strange boy as quickly as he could. No sane person would live in the saint's head. He handed over the prescription, said the course of treatment would last ten days and gave Samuel a few boxes of free medicine samples. He looked over at the door, wishing the two of them were already on the other side of it, but they didn't move a muscle.

"St Anthony has sent you a message, Dr. Adriano."

Dr. Adriano sighed but waited for more.

"He said a girl's going to come in here today saying she's got a pain in the heart. St. Anthony asked me to tell you that she's the love of your life."

"That's a good one!"

"Listen to me, Doctor. She will be bringing you your sock."

Sock. The word struck the doctor between the eyes like a lightning bolt.

"When did he arrive?" the doctor asked Francisco.

"A few days ago."

"Before last Friday?"

"After Friday."

"How do you know about the sock?" he asked Samuel.

"The saint told me."

No one knew about the sock. It had disappeared from the doctor's car. The previous Friday he had left one of the doors unlocked and a single sock had vanished. Just one of the pair—it was the oddest thing. If it had been a real thief, he'd have stolen the envelope of money that was in the glove compartment, his jacket, the car stereo, his watch, his bag. Candeia had never been the sort of place to have thieves. Getting a single sock stolen from a pair—that was something you didn't forget.

The doctor was shaken. He threw the two of them out of the room and hurried back to his desk. There was still time for Samuel to give Madeinusa an encouraging wink.

With every minute that passed during his work, the message from the saint troubled the young doctor more and more. This wasn't the kind of thing that happened in his predictable life. Every day he would wake up and drive his car to the towns where he worked, knowing precisely the menu of ailments that he would find. A message from a saint—that was not on the list. It was unsettling.

The most practical thing would be for him to stick his head out of the door and take a look at the queue, but he was afraid. With each woman who came in, his panic increased, particularly if it was a woman without many teeth or a hefty woman with digestive troubles. The rest of the patients were all men and children.

The young doctor rushed through the consultations as quickly as he could, sweating. He asked his assistant at the door how many people were still in the queue.

"Only three, thank God. I'll be out by eleven."

Two patients dripping with sweat and then finally Madeinusa. The long wait had left both of them overcome by anxiety—knowing that there was some superior force at work in this meeting. Hers were eyes of curiosity and courage. His, of dread and eagerness. Adriano was shy, very shy, especially when it came to women. Madeinusa had never been this close to a man in her life. Especially not in a room with no one else there.

She didn't even sit down. She took the sock out of her top, from the neckline of her blouse, and squeezed it tight in her hand. Meanwhile, he pointed toward the examination table, an iron thing painted in beige, old and peeling like everything else in that town.

Madeinusa climbed the iron steps and sat on the bed, because something told her to do this. The doctor took hold of his stethoscope nervously, already knowing that the ailment was in her heart.

Adriano, the timid doctor, brought the end of the stethoscope into contact with the girl's young skin and listened as she held out the sock and said:

"It's just . . . I've . . . I've got a pain in my heart."

Nothing else needed to be said for a romance to begin right then, a romance blessed by St. Anthony. Those who are shyest are the wildest when they attack, and Dr. Adriano kissed Madeinusa without even asking her permission. He had no need.

The health assistant must have heard the racket of the iron bed banging against the wall, and she soon flung open the door and saw the doctor examining Madeinusa with his hands and his mouth, without glasses, in order to see better. They barely noticed their audience.

It didn't take long for the talk to reach the ears of Helenice, a former devoted churchgoer, now a devout evangelical, chronically bad tempered, intolerant and prejudiced, miserly and hysterical mother to a deflowered young woman. And thanks to the message from St. Anthony, Madeinusa and Adriano soon set the date for their marriage, as Helenice didn't want a daughter with a reputation. Either, stated Helenice, the doctor married her and took on her dishonor, or Madeinusa was better off dead, in the name of Jesus Christ, hallelujah.

CHURCH

Madeinusa's friend—who did owe her money but had never won on the lottery—was the girlfriend of Aécio Diniz, whose slogan was "He tells it like it is." Aécio was a presenter on Canindé Radio 89.1 FM and got in touch with Madeinusa less than a week later, interested in learning more about this story of the message from St. Anthony. They set up an interview for the Bride of the Week slot, which had been a great success in the area, though it had been canceled several times recently due to a lack of brides. Those were difficult days for the romantically inclined.

Canindé was in full pilgrimage season, full of devotees of St. Francis like the ones Samuel had met on the road. There were many of them, thousands of them. Madeinusa put on perfume to speak into a microphone for the first time.

She told the whole story: that more than a year ago she had tied up St. Anthony under her bed, wrapped in cardboard, hidden from her mother, and prayed for help in getting married to Adriano, the doctor who didn't even know her.

"But isn't it forbidden to keep an image of St. Anthony in Candeia?" asked the reporter.

"It is, but I managed to get one in secret from the mother of a friend. She's going to be the matron of honor. And the best man will be Samuel, who brought me the message from the saint."

The program was broadcast in Canindé and a number of other nearby towns. Everybody stopped to listen when Madeinusa said that the outsider had heard the thoughts of St. Anthony because he lived inside his head. The episode with the stethoscope also got the attention of the listeners. Naively, Madeinusa recounted it all, repeated it, gave details. Never had Canindé Radio 89.1 FM had so many listeners.

Madeinusa's wedding dress was loaned by the beauty parlor owner, who'd worn it for her fifteenth birthday party. It looked as good as new; they just had to leave it out in the sun for a few days to get rid of the musty smell. It was white and puffy, with fake mini-pearls sewn all over it. It was so beautiful that it didn't fit into Madeinusa's little dreams. She had to learn to dream bigger.

Dr. Adriano was no less happy. He scraped together his savings and paid for the wedding party willingly. The biggest expense was doing up the little church of St. Anthony in Candeia; the two of them insisted that the wedding should be held there, in the remains of a town that meant so much to them.

The door to the little church had been locked with a rusty chain ever since Father Zacarias had been driven out, ever since that sea of misfortune had swept over Candeia. The old parish priest could barely believe it when Adriano's car pulled up outside his house in Tauá and he asked him to officiate at the wedding. He had baptized Adriano, Madeinusa and almost everyone who was still holding out in Candeia. The doctor told Father Zacarias what had happened, and about Samuel, the outsider. The priest looked up to heaven, utterly convinced.

"A miracle from St. Anthony! He may take his time, but he never fails!"

They painted the church inside and out. It was small; not even thirty people could fit inside it. They brought in laborers from nearby towns. The floor was washed more than four times, scrubbed till the brooms were ruined, and the benches coated with varnish and a lot of poison against the termites, which didn't think to spare a house of God.

Despite the evidence of the apparent miracle, the people of Candeia still believed that St. Anthony brought only misfortune, and no one wanted anything to do with this change. They still nurtured a hatred for the saint who had betrayed them, who hadn't even been strong enough to prevent his own head being left on the ground, far from his body, like any old decapitee. If St. Anthony was so powerful, why did he not make the impossible possible? Why would he allow such misfortune to happen? Those who remained in the town had turned away from Catholicism and learned to love images that had nothing to do with God.

"This is the work of The Enemy!" cried Helenice, who would not refer to Mr. Satan by name.

Adriano got hold of a suit for Samuel, the best man. A

suit, tie, shoes, eau de cologne, socks and underpants. He made sure Samuel had a bath, inviting him to his own house to scrub off every last dot of grime. And he even paid for him to get a haircut with the same barber in Canindé who had done the bride's hair. They arrived at the ceremony together, in the same car, under the alert gaze of the curious onlookers, who had been waiting at the door to the church for hours.

Madeinusa was beautiful. Adriano was moved. Samuel, unrecognizable. Now it really was possible to see how handsome this outsider was. In the little church the crowds of women jostled for a glimpse of the saint's messenger. Apart from the priest, the groom, the best man and Francisco, there were hardly any men at the ceremony. Those who reported back later said that there were sixty-four women.

Adriano came out of the church carrying the bride in his arms. She threw the bouquet of plastic flowers, which was pulled apart by a number of women and transformed into several treasured relics of the first new miracle of St. Anthony of Candeia, through his intermediary, Samuel, the carrier of the messages of heaven.

PART TWO

COMMERCE

Madeinusa and Adriano were the embodiment of people's hopes and prayers, and the women who had been at the wedding spread the word that there had indeed been a romantic miracle—a miracle that had joined this man and wife.

The details of the miracle got around, too: the head of the saint, the messenger, the consultation, the wedding, the honeymoon. The local girls pictured the newlyweds in a hotel on the beach in Fortaleza, running happily along the edge of the sea that Madeinusa would be seeing for the first time and swearing their eternal love. They imagined Adriano and Madeinusa concluding what they had begun when Dr. Adriano had first placed his icy stethoscope against Madeinusa's burning skin. There would be nothing to stop them: not the wrath of the mother of the bride, not the opposition from the groom's family—a trained doctor marrying a girl with practically no education. Their situation was all due to the saint.

The girls sighed. They yelled as though hysterical. They were in agonies of envy. They wanted to find love, too.

And each time they told the story, new details made the wedding a supernatural event. They said that St. Anthony had appeared to Samuel and whispered his messages, that the spirit of the saint had entered his body, acting through him. The story spread from woman to woman like wildfire, covering a bigger and bigger area, right into the middle of the pilgrimage to St. Francis in Canindé. The next-door town was full of people, and what should have been a period of faith and prayer was transformed into a carnival of frenzied women as they heard the message of hope from the wedding saint so close by. Their plans for faith, contrition and self-sacrifice drastically changed course.

Although Samuel had planned to leave his home in St. Anthony's head as soon as his leg was fixed, he found that it wasn't that easy. The voices kept him there, kept talking to him. They came not just in the morning and evenings now but at other times, too.

The day after the wedding, Samuel was woken before five in the morning, dazed with the clamor of women praying. There were six or seven that day. A dozen on the next. Another twenty on the third, and within a month there were more than he could count. It was no longer possible to differentiate one from another, nor to hear the voice of that one sweet singer as clearly as before. The women revealed that they'd tied the saint beneath their bed, buried him in the yard, dunked him in a bucket of water—and that they would only release him from his punishment after they had won the man they loved.

Samuel's habit on waking had been to move lazily up to the top of the head, where he could hear the Singing Voice. There he would stay, all day long, listening to the one voice that never prayed, never asked for anything. It just sang, sometimes at different times of day. Samuel had not realized, not yet, just how much listening to the singing had become an addiction, as vital as breathing, the only joy in his life, which had so little hope. But it was just when he most needed it—when he most wanted to spend the whole day thinking about recent events, listening to the Singing Voice and deciding when would be the best time to leave town, if he could force himself to do so—that things changed in the head of the saint.

Suddenly it was different. The voices weren't just coming from within the concrete, as he saw when he pulled back the curtain he'd put at the neck of his saint's-head house and looked outside. He didn't get a chance to count them, but he guessed there were already more than forty women there. Two of them were approaching on their knees, and some of them sped up when they saw that Samuel was at the makeshift door.

Within seconds the spinsters had invaded the head of the saint, kissed Samuel's hands, showed him the photos of the men they loved and asked all at once what they should do. Some of them knelt, a couple of them crying at the emotion of it all. Yet they kept coming into the home of St. Anthony's messenger, and when there were twelve of the desperate women trampling Samuel, touching the concrete, talking, shouting and crying, a strange vibration made the head of the saint begin to shudder. At first the women seemed to feel nothing and just kept on coming in. They looked at the scribbles, the names, the arrows, frowning in confusion; they talked and talked, and the head kept shuddering. Samuel felt as though the shaking was in his own body, that bit by bit the head was turning into a strange extension of himself, linked to him by that absurd ability to hear the prayers and music.

Meanwhile, in the little church of St. Anthony, Father Zacarias was about to ring the parish bell, which, having been silent for so many years, he had restored to once again wake the town. He had planned to do six peals of the bell; the crowds running toward the head of the saint stopped him.

Samuel was already desperate, hemmed in by women who trod on his mattress, knocked over his belongings, broke off bits of the head to take away as concrete relics (later, in some cases, even selling them) and kissed his hands. He was getting more and more alarmed at the trembling he had never felt in his house before. Father Zacarias arrived at just the right moment and, realizing the poor boy's alarm, ordered all the women out—out of a place he had not yet been inside himself.

The women did as the priest told them. All Catholics fear figures of religious authority. He told them to wait outside and say the rosary to St. Anthony.

Father Zacarias went into the head, which was still shuddering. He tried to talk to Samuel, but with each question the intensity of the shaking increased. It lessened slightly with silence, then increased again as he spoke, till it was possible to feel the ground near the head trembling, too.

Outside, all the women were kneeling and saying the rosary when yet another band arrived from Canindé, shouting and running toward the head. All Samuel wanted was to listen to the song—the song that he hadn't been able to hear since the women had arrived—and this seemed more important than his fear of another invasion.

Now more than fifteen women ran into the head as though they were entering the Pearly Gates. The head's shuddering increased significantly, and the priest finally understood what was going on.

"Oh, sacrilege! St. Anthony has a migraine!"

There was a great commotion. The saint's head was pulsing more strongly on the left side. That was it; all that trembling made sense now.

Francisco arrived at the same time, and he couldn't believe his eyes. He saw a sea of women surrounding the head of the saint, a bewildered Samuel, the priest trying to calm everyone down, women fainting. It was the hot sun, the heightened emotion. And there was no point in Francisco asking them to leave, because they had no intention of budging. On the contrary, there were more and more of them arriving, showing not the slightest intention of leaving the miracle worker's side until something happened.

Francisco was flabbergasted. It was too ridiculous to be true: Candeia, once again, was full of people. He fetched his father, who returned with him to the head. (As a gravedigger he didn't have much to do, since the few people in the town died slowly.)

“These people are going to need places to sleep,” said Chico the Gravedigger, as kind as ever.

They improvised some tents with twisted tree trunks and old sheets from the abandoned houses. They found water coolers, jugs and pans and filled them with water for all the pilgrims.

The saint’s head hadn’t stopped trembling. In the crowd was a medicine woman, and she made the region’s most effective herb syrups. It was said she had even cured a minister in Brasília of cancer. The priest asked her to help the saint get better. “If only we had a little fire to make him some tea, the poor thing . . .”

Samuel had an improvised stove, so he began to boil water.

Seemingly from nowhere, the medicine woman found the cinnamon and other ingredients that were now smoking in the pan. She climbed up onto the saint’s chin and threw the foul-tasting liquid into his gigantic mouth.

“Isn’t there a big cloth we can use to cover his eyes? In this hot sun a migraine will only get worse,” she called from her perch on his nose, where she was now massaging pork fat between his two huge eyes.

Francisco and his father arranged four sheets and blankets, also taken from the abandoned houses, to cover his eyes. Samuel gave him another dose of tea, and bit by bit the vibrations began to abate. It was already nearly noon when the women asked whether there was somewhere nearby that served food. Only Helenice’s place, Francisco replied. The women went there, but their journey was in vain.

"I'm not serving anyone who's come here to trouble Candeia. That there's the work of The Enemy, and God protect me from being any part of it," said Helenice.

"But we've got nothing to eat!"

"You can starve to death as far as I'm concerned. You're not getting a grain of rice out of me."

Only later did Samuel let out a little laugh when Francisco told him about this bit of defiance on Helenice's part.

"Leave it to me. I know how to persuade that poisonous snake."

The news that these women were surrounding the saint's head in search of a love miracle attracted the Canindé radioman again, who went over to record interviews for his show.

Seeing Aécio Diniz's big car with the trunk open gave Francisco an idea. Francisco persuaded the driver to take him and his father to buy food in Canindé. There would be rice, green beans, onions, coriander, curd cheese, dried beef. A good stew would assuage everyone's hunger nicely.

They soon returned with the ingredients and asked Francisco's mother to take charge of the catering. They took over the kitchen of the old Candeia school, which had been out of action for many years. Father Zacarias had kept the key. It was the door he had been sorriest to close. The few children who'd stayed behind had gone to school in Canindé. But now the men took turns at repairing and cleaning the place to get rid of all the bugs and plants that had invaded. They fetched firewood and set everything up in the kitchen as best they could—at least enough to prepare a meal.

"Resurrection," the priest was saying.

Around four in the afternoon, two huge steaming pans of stew were carried out to the front of the school and served on the plastic plates they had found inside.

"It's one *real* for each plate of stew!" said Francisco with confidence.

"You're going to charge these people for food?" complained the priest.

"If I don't charge them, how am I expected to pay for what I bought in Canindé, Father? The man let us have it on credit, but we agreed that I'd return with the money tomorrow."

What Francisco managed to get from the women who ate the St. Anthony stew, as he called it, was enough to pay off the debt and buy more food for the following day. He and his father also bought two tanks for storing water to sell at ten cents a cup, and they used plates, cups and cutlery from the abandoned homes of Candeia.

Francisco and the radioman formed a partnership. Bit by bit the area surrounding St. Anthony's head became a small pilgrim village. Samuel, confused and disturbed, remained in the head, trying to hear the Singing Voice that had disappeared in all the commotion. He had lost his music, the sweet singing, and he couldn't bring himself to leave before he knew who had made it.

Whilst supervising the reopening of the school kitchens and ministering spiritual support to the faithful, Father Zacarias sensed that Samuel was in great need of his guidance. While the women respected his orders not to invade the head of the migraine-prone saint, the parish priest talked to Samuel about the miracles, trying to understand what was going on. He wanted to know more about Samuel's life, to understand where his gift had come from, but as he started to listen for the first time, Francisco appeared.

"You're a genius!" Francisco said to Samuel. "Look what we've done!"

"I didn't know it would all happen so quickly."

"But it did, and I've already made a tidy profit today."

"You'd better split that with me."

"Are the two of you planning to make money from the miracles of the saint?" asked Father Zacarias.

"The parish will benefit, too, Father," replied Samuel, who had grown up learning how to handle the priests in Horto.

It was Francisco's father who thought of asking one of the Canindé artisans to go back to making statues of St. Anthony to sell. It had been forbidden, but that was before the miracle. Now everybody wanted one.

Expedito, the artisan, went to see the saint's head to draw the details so that he could make his just the same. That was when he noticed, hidden in a corner, the letter *M* in a circle.

"And what's this?"

"I don't know. Can't be anything important," replied Samuel.

All the same, the saint maker recorded the letter and the circle in his drawing. He returned to Canindé quickly: with any luck he'd have a clutch of saints to sell the following day.

The only people who ever joined Samuel inside the head

were Francisco, Father Zacarias and Expedito. The women waited anxiously for a word from Samuel, who was uneasy, torn between taking advantage of the thriving trade, thinking what to do about all those women and feeling sorry, very sorry, that he couldn't hear the Singing Voice in the midst of all the noise. By now he was desperate to know who it belonged to.

Fortunately for him, Francisco had an eye for a good opportunity and spotted the potential in one spinster's desperate appeal: "I want to talk to the saint's messenger—I'll pay anything!"

It was as if she'd spoken some magic words. Francisco didn't know precisely what to do, but Samuel would certainly be able to put together a plan.

COMMUNITY

Candeia was reborn. It was brought back to life by the hands of the faithful women who worshipped around the head of the saint, lit candles, prayed day and night and waited for a chance to talk to the messenger. They wanted to get married. Almost all of them had a secret love hidden in their hearts, sometimes even a forbidden one, but a love of some sort. Others didn't even have this. They had no focus for their prayers, no particular beloved for the saint to bring to them, but they wanted to get married because, out in the backlands, a woman who doesn't marry is a cactus without a flower.

Then came the men, brought to the head of the saint by their curiosity. Aécio Diniz got more slots on Canindé Radio and talked about nothing else. The more people who came to Candeia, the greater the profit for Samuel, Aécio and Francisco, impromptu partners in that enterprise.

Everyone, without exception, was shocked at the state of neglect Candeia was in. Many had thought no one lived there anymore. Before Samuel's arrival, only a few of the houses were inhabited. Some men decided to break in and occupy the empty ones, cut back the forest that had grown around and inside them, hang lamps outside, take the hammocks to be washed in the lagoon behind the hill. Many went to fetch their families from Canindé and the surrounding towns.

A few of the houses weren't as empty as they looked; their owners were still inside—dead. Chico the Gravedigger had had no idea that these corpses existed; he'd assumed that everyone had left rather than died here. Now he identified each body by his or her house, sometimes by the boots they had been wearing or the locket on a necklace. It would be impossible to identify anyone by anything else, as the bodies no longer had faces.

The gravedigger made a point of giving a modestly dignified burial to every newly discovered body. He asked the new occupiers to bring the images of the saints from the oratories in each house so they could be buried with their forgotten owners. Then they were buried with Father Zacarias's blessing and called by their names, and the customary Mass was celebrated for each of them, seven days after their burial.

Besides the priest and Chico the Gravedigger, nobody else was interested in the bodies. They just wanted to occupy the houses, to remake the town.

Those who had no families used the larger houses to sell a night's sleep for five *reais*. Hammocks were brought in from neighboring towns—admittedly at inflated prices, since by now everybody knew that Candeia had been brought back to life.

There was absolutely no order to this activity. Candeia did have a mayor and a chief of police, who were actually father and son, but they only ever showed up occasionally, to pay the caretaker at the town hall, the cleaner at the police station and the health center assistant. Dr. Adriano was paid by the state government. They'd have a quick glance at the town, with the mildest look of contempt they could muster, and would leave again without a trace.

Sometimes the mayor, Osório, would come to his house on his own, in the late afternoon. The house was one of a few he had in the area, but he preferred not to live in this one in Candeia and paid the town hall caretaker to maintain it. He'd park outside the house and spend the night there, dealing with the official municipality paperwork, and then leave. He didn't have the slightest interest in the problems of the people of Candeia. Last time the townsfolk tried to tell him something, he didn't come back for four months—and so didn't release the paltry payment to the town's three pensioners in that time. No one said a word, he didn't get annoyed and Candeia died away.

The activity continued at full pace. The biggest trade was in food and images of the saint. Father Zacarias stayed close to the head as much as he could, to try to understand what was happening, and blessed the statues people brought there, which encouraged sales.

Francisco and his parents had never seen so much money.

The radioman, Aécio, was endlessly announcing on Canindé radio supposed miracles performed by the head of the saint. It was like hypnosis—people just kept coming, more and more. Some of the houses in Candeia had their facades painted, and shop signs reappeared: "St. Anthony Hostel," "St. Anthony Snack Bar," "St. Anthony Barbers."

Even though he had yet to hear the Singing Voice again, Samuel kept his resolve to run away. This was not what he was in Candeia for—he had come following his mother's instructions.

Samuel said he was tired. Until not long ago, his life had been about making money at the expense of the faithful Juazeiro pilgrims: singing prayers to Father Cicero, as a guide on the Santo Sepulcro road, selling hats and petitioner ribbons, taking photos of tourists. His greatest dream had been to live as long as possible with Mariinha, have a laugh with his friends in Juazeiro, go out with the young Horto girls, sell hats, sing some prayers. But this dream had died with his mother. Then all he had wanted was to get to Candeia, see his grandmother, meet his father and then kill him, if he had the nerve. It wasn't looking likely. Old Niceia, his grandmother, was so fierce that no one had gone near her house. Samuel hoped that someone would and that they'd find his father inside—dead or alive.

"Can you still hear the voices?" Francisco asked Samuel.

"It's harder now. Before, when it was quiet round here, I could hear them nice and loud. Now I can't even hear the singing girl—there's too much noise, too many women talking. Though there was one day when I heard Helenice, at four in the morning."

"What was she saying?"

"Asking for forgiveness, asking God that all this not be a punishment, *mea culpa, mea maxima culpa,* asking that He watch over Fernando's soul."

"Right, Fernando was her husband. He died—it was his heart."

"But I don't think it was. She says she's full of remorse, that if she could go back in time she wouldn't do what she did, that her life would be better with Fernando, that she should have gone with him."

"I'll ask my dad if he knows anything. You think she poisoned the Portuguese man's fruit juice?"

"Her husband was Portuguese?"

"Yeah—and they say Madeinusa is as beautiful as she is because she's the spitting image of her dad. But we'll work all that out later. For now I want to know if you've got any plans to perform miracles for these women."

"I won't be able to do what I did with Dr. Adriano for all of them. It was easy when I didn't hear so many voices. Now it's tough. I've got one who's in love with a southerner from Caxias do Sul, and I don't even know where that is—how am I supposed to sort that out?"

"You just have to say the saint is going to help, but don't make promises. Come up with some prayer or other for them, the sign of the cross on their forehead, whatever."

"I think our best way out would be giving them a time

frame, saying it will only work after forty days. By then I will have gone."

Francisco's expression changed to one of shock and sadness.

"Gone?"

"Wasn't that the deal? My leg would get better, and I'd go. I've already stayed much longer than I planned. I came to look for my father, and I've realized that I'm never going to find him."

"But we're friends. You could get yourself a house to live in, a long way from the head. Just come here to work, like going to the office. Your father must be dead; best forget about him."

"The only reason I haven't left is because of the Singing Voice. I want to know who it belongs to."

"And what if she's one of those women outside?"

"She never prays, she only sings. She's sweet, and peaceful. There's no one like her in the world. She's nothing like those marriage-crazy ones outside."

"You can't know without checking. Can I announce that the consultations start tomorrow?"

"Yes. But also say they'll only last two minutes, because the saint gets a migraine if he works too hard."

"I'll charge two *reais* per consultation. Do you reckon that's a sin, Samuel? Do you reckon we should ask Father Zacarias?"

Samuel sighed, resigned to going along with his friend's plan. He knew Francisco needed the money. "I'm sure even God doesn't know what a sin is anymore, let alone the priest."

CAXIAS DO SUL

Samuel thought through how the consultations would work: he would receive each of the women inside the head, ask her to tell him the name of her intended—if there was one—and ask her to write the name on a piece of paper, which he would then rub on the right-hand side of the head. If the girl had no object for her affections, her own name would do, but in that case he would rub it on the left. The choice of sides was only to give an impression that there was some method to what he was doing, but it was no more than killing time. After rubbing the piece of paper, he would announce that the effects could take up to forty days. Within two minutes the consultation would be brought to a close. They would bring in between thirty and forty *reais* per hour, which wasn't bad, not bad at all.

They decided not to explain their scheme to Father Zacarias, who might ask questions and complicate everything. All they told him was that the saint had asked that all weddings be carried out in Candeia's little church—the women were told this, too. That way the priest was happy, and if he knew anything more about their moneymaking plan he didn't let on—dealing with the saint was the messenger's job.

The first three days of consultations were tiresome for Samuel, who had to repeat the same things over and over again, answering the women's anxious questions, explaining that it might be a while before anything happened.

With some of the women, the conversation went slightly differently. One girl had such pestilential breath that Samuel needed to ask for some incense from the church before he could breathe comfortably in his house again. Besides the ritual of rubbing the piece of paper on the head, he told this girl to find a chemist's urgently to buy herself some toothpaste and two brushes: one for her teeth and one to scrub her tongue.

Another girl, who was hugely fat, had leaned back against the side of the saint's head and made the poor thing roll over till his nose was almost in the earth. She'd had to lean on the opposite side to right it. Samuel made up an instruction from the saint that she must eat nothing but pineapple for a fortnight in order to purge herself of her sins, and that she must walk daily from Candeia to Canindé to light a candle to the saints, Anthony and Francis, who during their lifetimes had been friends.

Bit by bit Samuel began to embellish the advice he gave. Francisco looked after the queue and the collection of the money. Aécio Diniz took charge of selling the statues of the saint, the medallions, T-shirts and other bits and pieces, besides devoting practically his whole radio program to the latest events in Candeia. The proceeds were divided between the partners, under the supervision of Chico the Gravedigger, who couldn't add two and two but was a very honest man.

Francisco did his best to fill the consultation schedule for the whole day so they could earn as much money as possible. When the forty days were up, the trick would be discovered, the town would unmask the impostor and Samuel would disappear—leaving Francisco to pose as a victim of the deception. Francisco couldn't think of a new plan for after that; it was best just to make the most of the present. Every night before going to sleep, Francisco thought how much he was going to miss Samuel when he left.

On the eleventh day after consultations began, the queue of women anxious for a paltry word from St. Anthony's messenger was surprised by the news that there would be a wedding the following morning. Samuel received an invitation via a messenger: he was to be best man. The bride was sorry not to have invited him personally, but she was busy getting her dress fitted. She insisted that Samuel had to be there at the altar, though he couldn't remember seeing the bride, Madalena, for a consultation.

But the truth was, she would have been hard to miss. Madalena was the obese girl—ugly, oily-skinned, slick-haired—who arrived in Candeia a short time later, fifteen kilos thinner, in a wedding dress. She was married in a well-attended ceremony to the love of her life: a former work colleague. Their romance had been interrupted when he'd been transferred back to Caxias do Sul, where he was born. The girl had been sure that she would never find anyone else like him—this man who didn't even answer her letters—until the day when everything changed.

Aécio Diniz invited the groom to be interviewed on the radio—which now had a studio in Candeia itself.

"So one day I was working and I thought about Madalena. There was a voice telling me to leave my life in Caxias do Sul and come here to be with her. I sold everything I had: a green VW Beetle, two loudspeakers and a karaoke machine. All I wanted was to be near her."

"So you arrived here in Candeia with lots of money?" asked the presenter.

"None at all. I spent it all on the tickets."

The bride took the microphone.

"He arrived rich in love and beauty—that's what matters in life."

The two of them wouldn't stop their passionate kissing.

Even Aécio Diniz shed tears at the testimony of the southerner who was so mad about Madalena. The girl revealed in this interview that Egídio had experienced that sudden and devastating feeling of passion the same day as her consultation with Samuel, the miracle worker. Father Zacarias, hearing the interview, called on Samuel to explain this miracle.

"I lied to this woman," Samuel confessed. "I deceived poor Madalena, telling her to eat fruit for a fortnight, to walk here, there and everywhere, and now I hear about this miracle. I don't do miracles, Father, nothing of the sort, I came to Candeia at the request of my mother."

"What did you feel when you talked to Madalena? Any dizziness, any light-headedness, some sixth sense? Did you feel anything strange?"

"I did. That day I had a stomachache. I was blown up like a balloon, full of gas. What's happening, Father?"

"I don't know, my child. None of the books I've read describe anything like it. But I shall pray to God to forgive you, for whatever it may be."

"I think it's best for me to leave. I wanted to go sooner."

"You want to leave?"

"Yes, I only came to look for my father, but I soon realized I'm never going to find him."

"So what kept you in Candeia?"

"The Singing Voice. It's a girl whose voice sings inside the saint's head, and I wanted to find out who she is. It's the only thing that makes me happy."

"Maybe it's just an illusion. The Devil is filled with cunning wiles."

By now there was electricity in Candeia, though the mayor had nothing to do with it; it was being taken from the lampposts along the highway. Still, the mayor was due to arrive at any moment, alarmed from hearing the news about how much had happened during his absence and in such a short space of time.

The second wedding took place. And a third, fourth and

fifth. All the women who had consulted the saint's messenger had then, inexplicably, found the love of their lives. Samuel was invited to be the best man for every one of the weddings, until Francisco explained to the brides that this would no longer be possible. There were three or four weddings a day, and he was needed at the saint's head for the consultations. The guests of all the happy couples helped to fill the town.

The owners of the recently established restaurants, hostels and cafés were only interested in their trade, filling their pockets with money, then redecorating the buildings to attract more customers. Now the town had houses painted in different colors, street lighting and a blue church, and the main square was being redeveloped.

One of the couples who celebrated their ceremony in the little Candeia church came from Baturité. They stayed in the town for their honeymoon, along with the bride's parents, who declared they had never seen anywhere so beautiful.

No one could understand why the family spent their whole holiday taking measurements of a small dark house that had all its windows bricked up and tidying and sweeping around it. The strangest part was when a car from a construction firm showed up and unloaded more than ten gallons of black paint.

"Black? They didn't get any other color? Must be for some kind of witchcraft," someone said loudly.

The couple went away for a few days. Enough time for those who were curious to go into the house and see what was going on. All the internal walls had been knocked down and everything inside painted black.

"It must be something satanic," said Gerusa, Francisco's mother.

"We won't let anything bad happen," said Father Zacarias, though he was fearful.

The couple returned early the next morning, before sunrise. They arrived with a van full of chairs, a large piece of unfamiliar equipment and a big black sign, which they hung above the front door of the house.

With the help of a stepladder, the father of the bride climbed up while his wife remained on the ground and handed him enormous white letters, one by one.

When day broke, people flocked to the house to read what was written there. Two short words: "Cine Rex."

CASABLANCA

A cinema in Candeia. Nothing at all to do with witchcraft or dark rites. The room had been painted black to provide perfect viewing conditions.

The couple set the opening for a week later. They still needed to arrange the seating, test out the projector and wait for the movies to arrive. On the day of the opening, showings would be free in order to attract a clientele, as a lot of people in the town didn't even know what a cinema was.

Aécio Diniz didn't waste a minute: he talked to the couple who owned it, Ary and Thelma, and arranged a partnership whereby he would promote the Cine Rex on his radio programs in exchange for free tickets to give away to listeners.

The cinema would show three movies over the course of a day, to audiences of small children, youths and adults. Despite some cheeky requests and anonymous letters, the couple was quick to announce that Cine Rex was a family establishment and would not be showing pornographic movies.

On the day set for the opening, the line was enormous. The screening room was ready, but there was a serious problem: most of the movies hadn't arrived. Ary and Thelma tried to explain to the residents that they would have to postpone the opening of Cine Rex. If they opened now, they said, they'd have to show the same movie three times in the same day.

"So be it!" said Madeinusa, who had come for the opening. "What's the movie called?"

"*Casablanca*," replied Thelma. It was her favorite.

From nine in the morning, then, to eight at night, the population of Candeia was transported to Morocco. Men and women of all ages came out of the cinema weeping over the love story of Rick and Ilsa.

Candeia became the world capital of romantic love, of marriages born of love and mad passion. Father Zacarias's wedding schedule didn't allow him a moment's breath. Rich couples and poor, they all came to marry in Candeia.

Finally the new movies arrived and Cine Rex was too small for the number of people who wanted to watch them. Even with new movies on offer, the public demanded at least one showing of *Casablanca* every two days. Ary was in charge of the programming. He had spent his whole life waiting for the day when he could retire from his work and devote himself completely to the cinema, the second-greatest passion of his life. The first was Thelma, his wife. The two of them divided up the cinema duties well. Ary looked after the program and the ticketing. Thelma helped advise Ary on the choice of movies and took care of the snack bar: Thelma's. Her cooking was a whole other sensation, and Candeia was introduced to an Italian dish that took the town by storm: Thelma's lasagna.

The only problem was that sometimes Ary got caught up chatting at the door and forgot to charge for tickets. Thelma, meanwhile, so loved the cinema that she would sneak in to watch the movies in secret and leave the lasagna burning in the oven. But these weren't big problems, and the cinema continued to succeed.

The new cinema was the second-biggest piece of recent news to spread across the airwaves via the velvet voice of Aécio Diniz. The radioman earned so much money from his undertakings that he bought a stake in Canindé Radio and funded the broadcast of his shows across a much larger area. That was how a journalist from the capital came to learn about the head of the saint, the miracle boy, the weddings, the cinema—the entire resurrection of the town of Candeia.

The journalist's name was Túlio, and he was well known for his investigative gifts and for his reports, which left no question unanswered. When he heard about the story of the head of St. Anthony he was intrigued by the one thing that everyone else had forgotten: why had the town been so neglected in the first place?

For his first few days in Candeia, Túlio moved anonymously, as though just another curious visitor. He lodged in

Dona Rosa's house—a woman who had a remarkable memory of the place, like a library archive. He learned much from Dona Rosa, and he was soon certain that there was something very rotten in Candeia's past. And the people needed to be told.

CORDEL

By the time Father Zacarias received a little printed *cordel* recounting the history of Candeia, copies of it had already spread through the town. It was not yet even nine in the morning and already all the town's inhabitants were walking around with the pamphlet in their hand.

It was entitled "The Head of the Saint," and it told the whole story of the place, ever since it had been a little village and later when it became a town, right up until the day it was condemned to death and later brought back to life with the arrival of Samuel, the prophet sent by St. Anthony to live inside his head.

A woodcut image on the cover showed the saint's head on the ground, with one of his tears becoming a river, and in the distance a man running away with bags of money.

It was not an innocent pamphlet. Whoever was responsible for it had intended to reveal truths about the past, which up until that moment had stayed hidden. In its verses and rhymes there was a serious charge leveled against Osório, the perpetual mayor, of having stolen a lot of money from the local coffers. It described his house in the capital, his luxurious cars, the jewels belonging to his wife—who, according to the pamphlet, was well treated so that she might never suspect the secret love affairs he was having in various towns in the region.

Soon afterward, an article with the same tenor of accusations was published in a newspaper in nearby Fortaleza. Journalists from the capital and from other states came to the small town, equipped to the back teeth with cameras to record evidence of this festival of absurdities. They tried to interview Samuel, who refused. He locked himself in the head as best he could, although he resorted to hiring security reinforcements to protect himself.

The townspeople were revolted by what they read in the pamphlet. They demanded that the mayor appear to respond to each of these accusations. Father Zacarias sent Mayor Osório a message asking him to come to the town.

As the spiritual guide of this ever-growing population, Father Zacarias had an obligation to confirm the facts in order to check whether they were anything but slander. But the old priest was sufficiently experienced and intuitive to know that nothing the pamphlet said was a lie. Osório had indeed bled Candeia dry.

Reporters kept arriving in their cars. Several towns sent correspondents, because everything in that piece of writing and in that town was an absolute gift for journalists. Aécio

Diniz hired a stand-in for his radio program and started to work exclusively as the town's press officer. The more publicity, the better for his show and the radio station. He was now a partner in the saint's-head consultations, in the retail of saints and candles, in Cine Rex and in sales of Thelma's lasagna.

The region's news bulletins had never been so lively. The cameras didn't miss a thing, going into houses and telling the dreadful stories of the bodies discovered when the recent arrivals had begun to occupy the town.

There were only two places the crews were unable to enter: the head of the saint and Niceia's house. Aécio Diniz was waiting for an offer from a major international broadcaster to sell exclusive rights to show the inside of the head. He arranged to have the place surrounded, protected by wooden posts, chains and security guards, preventing anyone who might try to approach. He was even planning to construct a dome made of bulletproof glass.

Niceia's house, on the other hand, was a quite different problem. There was no one preventing anyone trying to occupy it, but all the reporters and cameramen who tried to go in would be struck down with strange and sudden ailments. Vomiting, stomach pains, headaches, dizzy spells, fainting. After a while nobody was sure whether the illnesses came from some curse or from the fear of getting close to the place. That was until a brave cameraman from a São Paulo network arrived. He had worked in the Middle East and on the Bolivian border, and nothing scared him, he said. He chose a lightweight camera, positioned it on his shoulder and armed himself with a mask over his face, a torch on his forehead and a revolver at his belt. Arriving at the gate of the house, he wiped away the sweat from his face but turned back to the crowd watching the scene to give them a thumbs-up. The cameraman leaped over the iron gate without any difficulty. He walked through the garden, filming everything, his muttered words inaudible to the crowd though the whole world would hear them on television.

Before long he had pulled open one of the windows and climbed into the house, to the applause of the people waiting outside.

"I'll see what conditions are like and let you know when it's okay to come in," he said.

The other journalists prepared their cameras and microphones and moved closer to the iron gate, their eyes fixed on the window. Some of them waited for the São Paulo cameraman to say the word, but others were already in the garden when they heard a cry. The cameraman leaped back over the windowsill and ran from the house, followed by a pack of more than twenty mad dogs, barking and growling, ready to tear off a piece of anyone who got close. The onlookers who had been surrounding the house began to run, terrified. They climbed onto the roofs of houses, some of them firing shots and throwing stones, but nothing they did could stop the dogs' barking. It was a circus of monsters.

The dogs only calmed down when everyone was some distance from the house. After this traumatic episode nobody tried to enter Niceia's home again.

From that day on, the brave São Paulo journalist never

spoke another word. He was hurried to a hospital in Fortaleza, where he was interned until he recuperated from his nervous breakdown, the cause of which the doctors were unable to diagnose.

Samuel heard what had happened—it was the only thing anyone was talking about—but nobody knew of his relationship to the crazy old woman.

He thought about his arrival in the town, his wound, his conversation with Niceia. Nothing that happened to the journalists had happened to him. When he heard people talking about the mystery of Candeia's last inhabited big house, which was impossible to enter, he decided to go back there to try to talk to his grandmother. As well as wanting to see what else was inside, he wanted to inform her that he would be leaving town, and soon.

CAUTION

The world had changed a great deal for Samuel since he had arrived, barely alive, in Candeia. He no longer had the freedom to walk around where he wanted, whenever he wanted, without being followed by hordes of desperate women. If he was to go to his grandmother's house, he needed a plan. The day after he'd made the decision to visit Niceia, he announced that the saint had asked him not to talk to anybody, not to give consultations, and also that nobody should come anywhere near the head or pray to him before six p.m. the following day. Samuel waited there in silence so he could try to listen to the Singing Voice, calmly and clearly.

According to the made-up message from the saint, it would take a day to clean up the negative energies in the town. Anyone nearby could be harmed. Francisco spread the word among the people who were near the head, while Aécio broadcast it on his radio program. It worked. Samuel didn't tell his friends what he was doing, he just said he needed a rest, and some peace.

It was four a.m. when he went to his grandmother's house. As soon as he clapped his hands by the gate, Niceia opened the inner door and appeared. Samuel noticed the broken window and tried to see whether he could make out anything inside the house, but it was impossible. The camera was still there, lying on the ground. Nobody had been brave enough to go and retrieve it.

"Go away!" called Niceia firmly.

"I've just come to talk to you, I won't take too much of your time."

"I want to talk to you, too."

Samuel was surprised.

"Leave Candeia. There's danger coming."

"What danger?"

"You see what's happening in this town? You see these hordes of people, this chaos, those people from the television? It's all because of you. It's all your fault."

"It's not! I never asked the saint to let me hear his messages, I didn't even want to go there; it was you who sent me. . . ."

"It's your fault. You shouldn't have done what you did, and there are some people who feel such hatred—" The old lady broke off, then said more loudly: "There are some people who would kill you today if they could. You must leave. What day is it today?"

"Sunday."

"Then you'll leave on Thursday. That'll be enough time to sort things out."

"I don't know what to do."

"You listen clearly: on Thursday, before you leave, you've got to stop by here."

"Why?"

"To say goodbye. I'm your grandmother, child."

"You're my grandmother, but you've never even given me so much as a glass of water."

"You're the one who ought to be giving things to me, now that you've gotten rich by deceiving the people of this town."

"Is there anything you need?"

"I need nothing."

Samuel sighed. The conversation was as difficult as he could have imagined.

"Between now and Thursday you be really careful, Samuel, really careful, because this is going to be a difficult week. Watch out, because . . ." The old woman stopped talking, then went on: "There are people coming. I'll be expecting you on Thursday."

She slammed the door. Samuel hurried away and saw that there were indeed people already arriving. He walked with his head lowered so that nobody would recognize him. He ran over to the head. He wanted to make the most of the silence and say goodbye. He wanted to hear the Singing Voice, perhaps for the last time.

CHANT

There was nothing to stop him leaving Candeia that same day if he'd wanted to. He had enough money to go anywhere he pleased, even to travel by plane. No longer was he the poor, broken young man who had arrived in the town dirty, barefoot and begging for water and dry bread. He had prestige now, and money. He showered daily at Francisco's, he wore good clothes, went to the cinema, ate lasagna and slept on a spring mattress inside St. Anthony's head.

He could have left the head, too, and built himself a house just next door. If he didn't, it was because of the Singing Voice. If he hadn't yet left Candeia, fed up with the routine of consultations, lies and noise, it was because of the Singing Voice.

Even after everything that had happened—the miracles, the weddings—the Singing Voice had kept singing, at least twice a day, at five in the morning and five in the afternoon.

On the occasions when Samuel was able to hear her, he could tell she didn't speak Brazilian Portuguese very well. She used a mixed-up language, and Samuel didn't know whether the mixture was just an accent or whether it was a different way of singing.

There were four tunes, which she would vary. Sometimes she would sing the same song morning and afternoon. Sometimes she'd change. Samuel was able to hum along to each one of them, but he didn't really understand what they meant. He would catch the occasional word: "home," "heart," "farewell," "sea," "return," "far." The rest of the words seemed to belong to some other, strange language.

His plan to keep people away was still working, and early that morning he pressed his ear to the crown of St. Anthony's head and was able to hear the Singing Voice louder than ever.

The tune unlocked something in Samuel's chest, a drawer full of ancient dreams. There was a time when he used to dream. About the sea, for example. He dreamed about the day he'd take Mariinha to see the ocean for the first time and to find out whether it was true what they said about the water in the sea being salty.

So he liked it when the Voice sang about the blue sea. *"Vida de mar . . . ,"* it went, and he could understand that very well. He thought of the ocean, about his former desires, about the time in his childhood when his hopes were still alive.

The Voice sang of longing, and he thought more about Mariinha—but without sadness, because not all longing is sad. He was able to imagine his mother united with her whole family of women, women who foretold their deaths matter-of-factly, as if it was just another day.

Listening to the Singing Voice, he was able to be happy. Yet however hard he tried, he never managed to discover where it came from. The woman wasn't praying, so she couldn't be one of the ones who had come to his consultations. He would recognize her voice if she had, he was sure of it. It was a serious voice, hoarse and pronounced.

Thinking about the Singing Voice without knowing her face was unbearable. But now Samuel had a date to leave. Thursday. He felt he had to obey the order he'd received from Niceia, his strange, strange grandmother. Perhaps because he missed having someone to obey. Perhaps because he sensed that Mariinha, were she alive, would have told him to do the same thing. Go away, leave this place, this whole deception.

The Voice sang beautifully that day, at five in the morning and five in the afternoon, as she always had done. After six the crowd of women resumed their praying and it was no longer possible to hear anything clearly.

Samuel did not have many days left in Candeia, and in those hours of rest and solitude he was sure that he was in love, completely in love, with someone whom he only knew by her voice and those few words that lived in his heart.

He decided to ask Aécio Diniz for help. It was risky revealing all the secrets of the Singing Voice, but it was his only hope.

Aécio broadcast on his radio program that Samuel, St. Anthony's messenger, needed to talk to the woman who sang every day, at five in the morning and five in the afternoon. At first he thought about making up a story about there being a message for her from the saint, but Samuel changed his mind.

“I don’t want there to be any lies with her,” he said.

And he waited, nervously, for her to appear at his house at any moment.

CLOAK

It was before dawn on Monday when Samuel sensed somebody moving the curtain cloth. He thought it must be the owner of the Singing Voice, but it was a violent attack by a cloaked man who had come to bring him a message.

The man had been infiltrating the pilgrims for several days, but the only way for him to get access to the head was by disguising himself as a devotee waiting for a blessing for his love. He wore a St. Francis tunic, tied at the waist with a thick rope. This attracted no attention—he was just another stranger; there were people in town from right across Ceará. No one would ever presume that his purpose was to attack Samuel.

"Don't kill him or even hurt him—just give him a really good scare." The instructions from the man's boss were as clear as day. By the second day in the camp he had already seen that the best time for the attack would be around three in the morning, when Francisco wasn't there and most of the pilgrims were asleep in their tents.

The man pulled up the hood of his cloak. He removed the rope from round his waist, rolled it up in his right hand and pulled back the improvised curtain to enter the head of St. Anthony. He leaped onto Samuel's back like a frog. He quickly wrapped the rope round Samuel's neck. Unknown to him, the despair of not being able to breathe was precisely what Samuel feared the most.

"I won't kill you, saint-boy, I won't do that. I'd like to, but my orders are just to pass on a message. You're to leave Candeia tomorrow. By tomorrow night, got it?"

"Who sent the message?"

"Best not to try to guess. It'll just make things more difficult for you."

"I'm not afraid of Osório; you can tell him that from me."

Samuel gathered his strength and tried to react but received two well-aimed punches to his face.

"I charge a lot to pass on messages, saint-boy. And yours was very expensive."

He pulled the rope tighter, till Samuel groaned.

"I've said all I have to say. You sit quiet here till I've gone, and don't wake anyone up. You'll only make it worse if you shout, because I'm not here alone."

"Damn coward!" Samuel tried to say, filled with loathing, but he was suffocating, turning purple, and didn't altogether believe that he would survive the experience.

"If you don't do what you're told, well, I wouldn't mind that too much, actually. Because then my boss will send me back, and this time it'll be to kill you. And I'd like to put an end to the friend of this damned St. Anthony."

The last tightening of the rope lasted a few seconds; then Samuel was left unconscious. He woke up later, at five in the morning, feeling weak, but perhaps he'd only woken because the Voice was singing inside the saint's head, stronger than ever, in her incomprehensible tongue. Just a few words made it past the veil of that strange language to present themselves to Samuel. That day it was "courage"; she was singing about courage. She sang two lovely songs, in a rhythm that had seemed so strange at first but that was now so familiar to Samuel's heart. Then, finally, for the first time, the Singing Voice prayed. It was brief: "Give me courage, St. Anthony. I need courage, and strength." Samuel wanted to meet her at once, to ask her to pray for him, to ask her to take him in her arms and hold him like a child. He remembered Mariinha, remembered her as if she had been the one singing in that strange language. He cried. Ever since Mariinha's death he hadn't shed a single tear, but he cried now. Niceia's prediction was coming true; things were starting to get dangerous in Candeia.

Francisco arrived soon after five and was alarmed at the state Samuel was in.

"There was a man who came in here. I couldn't get a proper look at him; I don't know who he was. He tied a rope round my neck and said I had to get out of Candeia."

Francisco called two men into the head, and they picked

Samuel up in their arms. He needed rest, medicine—something to help his neck heal—and to be kept away from everyone while Francisco tried to understand what had happened.

There was nowhere Francisco's friend could be taken but the house of his father, Chico the Gravedigger.

PART THREE

CACHAÇA

Before the great misfortune, Candeia had been a lively place. The church was often packed with the faithful, who came to pray to the patron saint when his day came around. They would ask St. Anthony to bless their town.

On the clean white cemetery wall, women would practice magic rituals to get hold of a husband and find out what the man in question looked like. Young women would hurl eggs furiously against the wall and run over to see what pattern the yolk might make as it trickled down. They believed in everything, because hope and desire can make the impossible happen. The reputation of that wall raced from town to neighboring town and attracted the despair of many young women who were frantic to marry.

A speech from the mayor was traditional on the patron saint's feast day, but one year there was a rumor that the speech would reveal a huge piece of news for the town.

Nobody expected too much. Candeia was a peaceful place, really very peaceful indeed, with almost a thousand inhabitants spread along symmetrical streets, which had been minutely planned by the town's founders, along with their surroundings. No crime, no great upsets, no great townspeople, no serious problems. The mayor led the town with a firm hand and the help of a wife who was an absolute saint, as the women of Candeia used to say.

Considering this almost monotonous tranquility, no big bombshell was ever expected—so the rumor of any news in the official announcements seemed particularly curious.

The mayor and his wife climbed up to the platform. Someone adjusted the microphone on its stand, but the mayor was whispering something to one of his advisers and hadn't yet begun to speak. But now the eccentric young Father Zacarias was running toward them nimbly, climbing the steps to the platform two at a time and smiling like never before. He had recently arrived in the town and seemed to be full of new ideas.

"People of Candeia," began the mayor at last. "Good evening! We're all gathered here at this feast-day celebration to praise our patron saint, St. Anthony of Padua, the Portuguese nobleman who left our town as the greatest example of his passage here on earth . . ."

He gave a long pause. His lower lip was trembling. The mayor had learned this from an American film and thought it was lovely.

". . . his Christian, crystalline love. But I believe St. Anthony is not happy with us. In fact, I think our poor saint must be fed up with each and every one of you, people of Candeia." The audience exchanged appalled glances. The mayor went on, undisturbed: "How is it possible that a town that has St. Anthony as patron saint should go on despite the shame of not having a single big statue in his honor? Well, I have come to you today, people of Candeia, to announce that I have signed a contract with the firm of M.J. Engineering, which has built many exceptionally beautiful sacred monuments all over Brazil, to construct a twenty-meter high statue of St. Anthony to go up on the hill."

The townspeople were thrilled.

"We are going to make Candeia St. Anthony's third homeland. First comes Lisbon, where he was born. Then Padua, where he died. And now Candeia, where he has returned to live forever!"

Nothing that had ever happened before had awoken such a commotion in Candeia. Anyone who was not nearby when the speech began was attracted by the crowd. Fascinated, Candeians were delighted at the news.

"Along with the federal government, I have managed to secure authorization for a credit line for any entrepreneurs who want to set up a small business. Just look at Canindé, with so many people to shelter, to feed, to accommodate. Set up your inns, your restaurants, your little shops. Let's make Candeia prosper!"

The uproar was uncontrollable. Building a giant statue of St. Anthony was so impossible that no one else had even been able to dream of such a thing. The people expected the change to be quick and dramatic. The date for the unveiling of the statue was a year away—allowing enough time for the town to sort itself out and spread the word.

The new businesses began to spring up, with their names painted onto the fronts of houses: "St. Anthony Barber's," "St. Anthony Snack Bar," "St. Anthony Hostel," "St. Anthony Restaurant."

The promise of a successful new town attracted outsiders into Candeia. People interested in the new Candeia showed up from everywhere. They formed partnerships, but they weren't all successful. Some stayed, others were kicked out. But of all of these, none was a bigger hit than Fernando, a Portuguese businessman who was passing through the backlands and who smelled prosperity in that place.

Fernando sold fabrics and traveled the whole world. He dealt in cloth, from small pieces to large-scale orders. He negotiated between companies in São Paulo and Senegal, traded lace from Ceará for Chinese silk. He dispatched imported Indian saris to shops in Rio de Janeiro. And he spoke several languages. His talk was intoxicating, that's what they said. He couldn't get into a negotiation without the outcome ending up to his advantage, and he was always smiling, his almond eyes dancing as he spoke to his customers.

In a town full of young girls who were desperate to marry, Fernando's arrival had an even bigger effect than the announcement of the construction of the statue of the saint. For besides being a good talker, he was also very handsome. He had smooth black hair, always nicely combed back, attractive dark eyes and skin that was dark from so much sun.

Within a short space of time, the news spread that he

was betrothed to Helenice, daughter of the wealthiest man in Candeia—although this didn't count for much. No one had expected it. As far as anyone knew, the girl led a cloistered life and was soon to enter the convent in Baturité. She wore long skirts and her hair tied back—or at least she did until Fernando walked around Candeia Square with her. Now she let her hair hang loose in public, making respectful gestures and exchanging glances of love. Yes, she truly did seem very much in love.

The wedding was set for the following year, for the day after the unveiling of the statue. Fernando went away, claiming that he was going to buy white silk for the bride's dress—pure Chinese silk. His relatives were already packing their bags to travel to Candeia from Braga in Portugal. It would be the wedding of the century.

While everyday life went on all round the Candeia church, up at the top of the hill the saint's body was already in place, from his feet up to his neck. Anyone passing from the road could see it. The head, meanwhile, was still disassembled, its pieces spread around on the ground. This was the point in the work when the lead engineer of M.J. Engineering was called off to an urgent job in the capital and had to be away for a week. Before leaving, he called a meeting with the priest and the mayor and announced that in his absence he would be leaving the work in the hands of "Meticuloso," a local workman who had stood out for his intelligence. It was the engineer who'd given Meticuloso his nickname, awestruck at his natural tendency toward perfection, focus and attention to detail.

The engineer went away and Meticuloso couldn't help having a brief celebration with his friends. Barbecue skewers and cachaça. A lot of cachaça. The following day, the eight men charged with assembling the saint's head went to Meticuloso's house at seven in the morning and found him still drunk. They asked him what they were supposed to do to start the construction of the head—whether they should await orders or begin at once.

"I'm the one who gives the orders round here. Didn't you hear Mr. Engineer say so? You can put the head together on the ground, so that when he's back he'll find the whole saint finished."

The stonemasons spent a week assembling the skull, the chin, the neck, the eyeballs, the mouth and the nose of the saint. It was all millimetrically perfect, under Meticuloso's constant supervision. The inhabitants followed the progress of the face as it took shape, and there was a small gathering looking at the holy head when the engineer arrived. Meticuloso was so proud of what he had achieved that he took the liberty of marking the saint's head with his signature, the letter *M* within a circle.

Then the crowd parted to let the engineer through, who was shouting and yelling: "You idiot!"

CHRIST THE REDEEMER

It took him some time to get his anger under control, and he had to be calmed down by the people. The usually well-mannered, incredibly polite engineer got into a terrible state and wanted to give Meticuloso a beating. He wanted to kill the man, and only afterward was he able to explain why: the head should have been assembled right up on top, on the neck, with the help of some scaffolding that was on its way. He was almost sure that this head, assembled down on the ground, could never be carried up to the top of the saint's body.

His suspicion was confirmed by an expert who was brought over from Rio de Janeiro to assess the situation. The town hall didn't even have the money for the man's ticket, but the engineer paid for it out of his own pocket. It was the cost of rescuing a piece of work that could lead to prosperity or failure.

His name was Dr. Rubens, and everyone held him in high regard because he was part of the firm in charge of maintaining the Christ the Redeemer statue in Rio de Janeiro. His opinion would be definitive.

After a few days of examination, analysis, calculation and phone calls, Dr. Rubens gave his diagnosis. Carrying the head up to the body would be impossible. There wasn't a crane in the world able to bear that much weight. The only solution was to make a new head.

Dr. Rubens left and couldn't help giving a little laugh when he saw, from a distance, the headless body on top of the hill.

"Idiots."

The mayor had no more money to create another head; the local council had accumulated ridiculous debts, they were behind on their installments and there were no more creditors with any inclination to lend so much as a cent to anybody in the town. The unveiling party was canceled. News spread by word of mouth, because the mayor had gone to the capital, rarely to return, lacking the courage to face the people of Candeia.

Unhappiness. Misfortune. Despair.

Meticuloso, who'd been left in charge, vanished. All that remained was his signature, the *M* in a circle, recording for all time the man responsible for Candeia's ruin.

CHICO THE GRAVEDIGGER

The description of Samuel's injured neck, his one closed eye and the blood coming out of his nose spread very quickly around the pilgrims in the town and to everyone who was on their way there. It was nearly time for the pilgrimage to St. Francis in Canindé, and a lot of people took advantage of their journey to stop off in Candeia to ask St. Anthony's messenger for a wedding.

It was hard to keep in check all the people who accompanied Francisco as he carried Samuel to the home of his parents, Chico and Gerusa. They had to cross the cemetery to reach the little house on the far side. They had no choice but to close the cemetery gate behind them and secure it with a chain. It would only be unlocked when the inhabitants calmed down, which was taking some time to happen.

The efficiency with which the news spread meant that it didn't take long for Dr. Adriano to arrive, even though this wasn't one of his surgery days. He brought medical supplies, medicines and, most of all, his friendship.

"I still can't understand it," said the doctor.

"It must be Osório, Dr. Adriano. It was because of the pamphlet," Samuel replied in hatred. He wondered whether the mayor knew where Meticuloso was—the man responsible for the *M* in the circle on the head, responsible for the town's misfortune.

"I heard the rumors. The pamphlet is the one thing everyone's talking about everywhere."

"Osório must think Samuel is obstructing his plans," said Chico the Gravedigger. "People think he wrote the pamphlet."

"You've got to be really careful, Samuel. Best not go back to the head."

"Where am I supposed to go, Dr. Adriano?"

"You can come with me and Madeinusa, we'll work something out."

"You can stay here with us, hidden. It's safer here in the cemetery," said Gerusa, arriving with a plate of chicken broth for Samuel.

As he struggled to drink his soup lying on the sofa, everyone else sat at the table to have their lunch—Francisco with his father, mother and little sister, Diana. Dr. Adriano left, promising to come back the following day.

In the presence of the girl, they all changed the subject. They behaved just as they did on any other day, listening to her chatterings, laughing at nonsense, trying to keep things as light as they could.

The family all interacted with a natural affection and unpretentious love for each other, in their looks, their expressions. Samuel watched from the sofa, and his heart was split between gratitude at the welcome they were giving him and a deep sadness that he was not a part of that life, that he had no family of his own. No mother, no father, no siblings.

Outside there were hundreds of pilgrims praying for him. The rumors about his ailments grew and became increasingly sophisticated. Some said he had stigmata, the same wounds Christ had suffered on the cross, which only appeared on the chosen few, out of deserving and sanctity.

These rumors made the number of pilgrims and gawkers grow at an alarming rate during the day. They were outside, praying—which might have consoled Samuel. But it did not. Loneliness would be his forever. He was apart. There wasn't a single person to whom he could point and say, "They know all about my life, they're with me, they accept me, they are my family."

Mariinha had taken so much away with her. Her absence was too painful, but it was only now, nearly a year later, sitting on that torn sofa in the cemetery house, that Samuel understood that the wound in his heart was incurable.

He expected nothing from his grandmother Niceia. She was a crazy old woman, blind to the world, locked in the most sumptuous ruin in Candeia. And it seemed Samuel meant nothing to her, nothing at all. As for his father, Samuel was convinced now that he must be dead.

It was the most difficult day since Samuel had run down

Horto Hill and away from Juazeiro. Awareness of his solitude hurt more than any other pain.

Samuel managed to sleep in the afternoon, and when he awoke, Chico the Gravedigger was sitting beside him. Francisco and Gerusa had gone out to give news of Samuel's progress to the people who were gathered at the cemetery gate, and Diana was asleep in her room.

Chico's expression was very serious.

"I want to talk to you, now that we have a little time."

"What is it?"

"Leave this place, Samuel. Go away. Osório—if it is him—isn't messing around. Go somewhere very far away, somewhere he'll never find you."

"You really think he's as dangerous as that?"

"I'm sure of it. You've changed everything around here."

Samuel felt his eyes sting, and Chico the Gravedigger put his hand on his shoulder.

"I think he's the only person who hasn't been pleased that you came. You've brought us all a lot of happiness."

"Him and the witch Helenice."

They both laughed.

"I've never understood exactly how it was you came to be in Candeia. When I first heard about you, it was because of the doctor's wedding, and Francisco never said a thing to me about you. What brought you here?"

The subject of this conversation, Chico's manner, his tender voice . . . Samuel wanted to cry.

"I was living with my mother in Juazeiro, just the two of us. When she died, she asked me to come to Candeia to find my father and my grandmother so I wouldn't be alone in the world. But then I got here, I found the head and all the craziness started."

The piece of paper his mother had given him never left Samuel's pocket, but now he kept it in a leather wallet. He showed it to Chico: "When my mother died, this was all I had, this address in Candeia."

Chico asked the names of his father and grandmother, as he couldn't read.

Samuel said hesitantly, "Niceia Rocha Vale, Manoel Vale. With each syllable that Samuel spoke, Chico the Gravedigger's calm eyes were transformed and the most horrified, astonished expression Samuel had ever seen swept over his face. He got up without a word and went to get a drink of water. He pushed his hands through his hair.

At that moment Francisco and Gerusa arrived. Scared to see Chico looking so pale, they asked what had happened. Samuel answered that he didn't know, they were just talking when his friend's father had reacted like that.

"What's up, Dad?"

Chico the Gravedigger looked at Gerusa with tragedy in his eyes. "Samuel is Manoel Vale's son."

"Who's he?" asked Francisco.

It was the woman who had the courage to answer:

"Meticuloso."

CAPE VERDE

Before they had been married even six months, Fernando had announced to Helenice that he needed to go on a business trip and that it might take some time.

"But why on earth to Africa? It's an outrage!" She was crying as though she was about to suffocate.

"I'll come back, my dear, and if everything works out I'll be a rich man when I do!"

"Rich? How come?" The crying slowed.

"Because I'm going to buy fabric in Cape Verde. You can buy cloth from Senegal there, and Mozambique. Then I'll come back to Rio. There's a samba group who's promised to buy whatever I bring back."

"A samba group? So now you're going to Rio for Carnival, too?" The crying was back.

"Of course I'm not, woman. I'll be going long before that. They need the fabric to make their outfits. Trust me, I'll be coming back a rich man."

She had no choice but to trust, and to believe, and to hold back her tears when the time came to say goodbye. She knew what the people of the town were always saying about men whose work meant they spent a lot of time on the road. She assumed a serious expression, very serious, which she decided to keep until Fernando's return, to avoid any stupid conversation coming her way. She learned that being agreeable was just an open door to so many people. She was unpleasant, and she never invited anyone to be a part of her life. Within her house she wept rivers of longing for her husband. Before going to sleep, there were only tears, only lamentation. She worried about his not eating properly, about his health, about his clothes. She missed his dark skin, his accent, his hair, his eyes. Meanwhile he, on the other side of the ocean, wasn't missing a thing.

Fernando married Helenice because she was beautiful, because Candeia smelled of prosperity, because deep down he'd always wanted a home to return to. And above all, because he dreamed of having children, and Helenice's wide hips promised a good brood. But he found it hard to bear the fact that there was no room for anything in his wife's head beyond that little world of Candeia—who married, who died, who sinned . . . other people's lives—she lived without dreams, without trying new paths, as though that town were the whole world, when it wasn't. The world was huge, full of things, all of them far away from him. And in Candeia the worst thing of all: there was no wind. He needed to air his body, his ideas; he needed the wind on his face. And so he didn't think twice: Fernando went off to feel the wind in Africa.

He hadn't been lying: he really had gone to buy fabric for the Rio Carnival. As soon as he arrived in Cape Verde, the first thing he did was take off his wedding ring and hide it well. To begin with, his plan had been to stay about a month on the island of Santiago, awaiting the arrival of a shipment of fabrics from Senegal, and then return home. In his first few days there he befriended the owner of a little store in Sucupira, the enormous open-air market where all kinds of things are for sale.

Fernando spent his days at Sucupira looking at the fabrics of his competitors, trading the Indian silks he had brought with him, learning about the patterns on the African cloths and staring at the fleshy bodies of the Cape Verdean women, especially the body of Maria, the stunning owner of a stall selling necklaces and earrings made from volcanic stones.

Maria had caught his attention, standing out from the others, ever since his first day there. First because of her merchandise, those shining black beads that she used in her necklaces and earrings, and then because she always sang as she arranged her workplace. She'd arrive early, at five in the morning, remove the canvas sheet that protected her possessions from the inclement nighttime weather, and position her chair and the wooden trestle table. On a horizontal board lined with red cloth, she spread out her necklaces, earrings, bracelets. She would hang a few necklaces on the two wooden dummies, to catch the interest of passersby. She invented new designs for bracelets and earrings in that particular stone which shone more brightly than black pearls.

At five in the afternoon, as she took everything down

again to leave, she would resume her singing and cast a spell on Fernando's heart with her low, strong, sweet voice, articulating each word of Cape Verdean Creole with such pleasure.

He had been watching her for days, walking past, smiling at her. He tried to remember Helenice, but by this point she was no more than a wisp of smoke. One day he was unable to resist, and he went over to speak to the girl.

"What's that stone called?"

"It's *sibitchi*. It wards off the evil eye and attracts good luck," she replied in Portuguese, with the set phrase she always used with customers.

"Can men use it?"

"They can." She gave an ivory smile.

"Then I'd like a necklace, a really big one. I need a lot of good luck."

Maria had a long necklace there with her. As usual, she offered to fasten it at the back of his neck. When her hands touched the Portuguese man's skin, he felt capable of doing anything, anything in this life, to make that woman his, to make her sing just for him.

She had felt the same as soon as she saw him.

It wasn't long before Fernando had rented a house close to Sucupira and moved in with Maria. They expanded the store a little and sold *sibitchi* and fabrics—the ones from Senegal and the Indian silks he had left.

Maria liked to talk. She'd say, "Story, story . . . ," and would start to recount the legends she had known since childhood, of animals and people.

Fernando liked her talking as much as her singing.

Sometimes he would say, "Story, story . . . ," and he would tell Maria the love stories he had read in books.

Fernando had never been an early riser, but he got into the habit of waking at four-thirty in the morning to be with Maria and to listen to her as she sang, not saying a word, moved by the sound. Sometimes he even cried.

"I don't know why you cry."

"They're painful, those songs."

"It's called *morna,* this kind of singing. In this country people are born hearing *morna* songs, and we die with them, too."

"I want to die hearing you sing."

One day Maria woke earlier than usual, but she was unable to sing. She felt like throwing up. She asked Fernando to set up the things on the stall and take her to a prayer woman in Sucupira to get some medicine. The old lady was exact in her diagnosis: "You're pregnant."

And she was indeed. She got over the nausea and went back to work, singing as usual, stroking her belly. She gave birth to a beautiful little girl, whom she called Rosário. She looked just like her father. The same eyes, the same smile.

In that life of working at Sucupira, looking after the little girl, listening to *mornas,* time passed without Fernando realizing it. Things were good for him in Cape Verde. He had already started wearing the local clothes, he never took off the *sibitchi* necklace, he'd learned a little Creole and he was happy, soothed by the *mornas* that Maria sang. From time to time, she would sing *coladeiras,* happy songs, songs to dance to. He loved every note and lived for that voice.

Occasionally he would write a letter to Helenice, making up excuses for his delay in returning. He'd already been away from Candeia for nearly two years now and was considering never going back. He only sent the letters because Maria asked him to.

"You and she were married by a priest, it's a serious matter. Send her a letter from time to time."

"But I never want to go back there. There's no wind in Candeia. What I want is you, and my Rosário, and my Cape Verde."

"You'll have to go back one day."

"I didn't leave anything behind in that place, my love—if it were up to me, I'd never go back!"

"Never is like the moon—it belongs to nobody. Don't close the door to Helenice in your life."

Maria's words gained greater significance when the two of them decided to travel to São Tomé.

They went by boat. Fernando loved the sea, and it was Rosário's first trip on a boat. It was a lovely journey, all of it, especially when Maria sang *mornas* for the whole of the boat to hear.

When they were already very close to São Tomé, the craft struck a rock, the hull was punctured and it capsized. Rosário had been sleeping beside her father, who saved her as he cried out Maria's name. It was nighttime, impossible to see anything. The next day they found Maria's body close to the beach. She was the only person to die in the accident.

He had nobody to turn to in Cape Verde, nor in São Tomé. Maria had no relatives; she had been alone in the world.

Fernando didn't even contemplate returning to Portugal with the child; his family there would never accept her.

All that was left for him was to rely on Helenice's support and understanding in taking in the orphaned girl, since his wife had so wanted to be a mother. Fortunately Fernando managed to find his wedding ring. He remembered Maria's words, which had been a wise premonition. In Brazil he had a home, and a devoted wife who might forgive him.

He summoned up all his courage and went back to his wife. Old, downcast, defeated: his only joy was Rosário, the keeper of all Maria's beauties.

Fernando was all set to tell the truth, but he wasn't expecting to arrive home to find Helenice with a daughter in her arms, the fruit he had left in her belly before leaving. The girl didn't even have a name yet. She hadn't been baptized, nor had her birth been registered, while they waited for her father.

Fernando introduced Rosário as a lost child he had found in Cape Verde and decided to adopt. Helenice believed him, praised her husband's kindness and agreed to take the little girl in as her own daughter.

The two children became good friends. They were close in age and liked to play together, in spite of some differences in language and custom. Fernando immediately arranged the registration of his legitimate daughter's birth and her baptism. They called her Madeinusa.

After Fernando had been back home for a week, life in

Helenice's house seemed to have returned to normal. Fernando swore an oath that he would never travel again unless his family went with him. He asked forgiveness for the lack of news, for the lack of money, and he was relieved to learn that his father-in-law had died and left his only daughter his restaurant—it would make her a good income.

The two children became ever closer. They played together and slept together, and Fernando took care of them both all day long. Madeinusa thought it was funny when Rosário spoke to her father in Creole. She didn't understand a thing, but she saw the language as a secret spell, a treasure her sister had brought from the sea. Rosário liked to sing at five in the morning and five in the afternoon, just like her mother. With her father's help she was able to recall the words to the songs; he had memorized Maria's five favorite songs and took care to ensure that his daughter learned them, too.

Rosário frequently asked after her mother, but fortunately she did so in Creole and nobody understood. She called him "Father," but this didn't sound strange, since the idea had indeed been that the couple should adopt her as their daughter. Helenice spent her whole day at work and barely saw the two girls. During the night she devoted herself completely to being Fernando's wife, in all the ways she could, in order to get over those years she'd spent missing him.

Things started to change one Saturday when they decided to go into Canindé for an ice cream. They were commemorating the one-month anniversary of Fernando's return. Candeia's decline had already begun, and going out of town was the only leisure option its inhabitants had. The place was gradually becoming a ghost town.

The priest of the local parish, who hadn't seen Helenice in quite some time, praised the beauty of the two little girls and their resemblance: "The same eyes, the same smile, that same expression of their father's," he said. "Only the color of their skin is different, otherwise they're the spitting image. May God bless these two sisters, in the name of the Father, of the Son, and of the Holy Spirit."

As soon as she began to notice the similarities between Rosário and Madeinusa, Helenice tried to bat the thought away. It wasn't possible. A mother wouldn't surrender her child like that, unless it had been a kidnapping. However hard she had tried to ignore her suspicions, the atmosphere between her and Fernando became so fraught with tension that she found herself unable to sleep one more night without knowing the truth.

When the two girls had fallen asleep, Helenice asked Fernando whether Rosário was his daughter, and he didn't dare deny it. He told her the whole story, the tragic death of the child's mother, Maria's pleas that he never stop writing to Helenice. The more Fernando tried to explain, the angrier his wife became. It wasn't what he said, but the way he talked about that other woman, the misty look his eyes took on when he said "Maria." She'd never seen her husband talk like this about her, or about anything else in life, with that pained passion in his chest.

Even she didn't know the power of the sleeping hatred within her, of her shame, of the bitterness she felt when faced with that unforgiveable betrayal. Not because of the nights of passion they had shared, not because he had slept with that African woman, but because he still loved her even now, every second of the day.

She asked her husband if they could continue with the conversation the following day, as she couldn't bear to talk any more just then. Fernando was surprised at her reaction; Helenice always cried, she fell apart, but now she looked hard and frightening.

But there was more than that: she had a gun. She had bought it to defend herself against any drunks and thieves who might show up at the restaurant, and nobody knew of its existence. A lot of people had left Candeia by this time, and as her house was close to the road, she was sure nobody would hear a thing.

And indeed, nobody outside did hear the bang of the well-aimed shot to her husband's chest that killed him as he slept.

Madeinusa was a deep sleeper, but Rosário awoke in alarm. Helenice picked the little girl up and carried her out of the house, taking care that nobody should see her. She hated the child. She wanted to kill her, too. She took the girl out onto the road and told her to walk, because her mother was waiting for her just up there, over in that light—she pointed way off into the distance. Rosário was too young to know that dying meant never again, that her mother wasn't in that light, that Helenice meant to kill her—and only didn't because she didn't have the courage. Rosário smiled, sleepy-eyed, showing an expression of surprise and innocent joy in anticipation of the reunion.

"Run, Rosário! Run, see your mummy!"

As the girl ran, barefoot, Helenice pointed the revolver at her, but lowered her arms when she saw the little childish walk that looked so like her daughter's. The girls were identical. The same body, the same height, the same age. Daughters of the same father, the dead wretch who had destroyed her life.

She wanted to take Rosário up in her arms and carry her back home. She remembered her husband and became so confused that she no longer knew whether the shot had been real.

Rosário ran, ran up the road, calling for her mother. Helenice, meanwhile, ran back home. She asked God to look after the little girl. She didn't want to see her, didn't want to remember the disappointment that her existence represented. "Look after the unfortunate wretch, oh Lord."

She prayed till she got home. Fernando really was dead on the bed, his eyes open, a bullet in his chest and the wedding ring tight on his finger. It wasn't a hallucination. She had to act quickly.

What was left of the town of Candeia awoke to the weeping and wailing of Helenice, who was on her way to the church, calling for Father Zacarias.

"Fernando has had a heart attack!"

That was the official announcement of his death. When the first people reached her house, the dead man was already nicely laid out in the coffin, in a jacket, his hair done and smelling of cologne.

Helenice asked for the burial to take place quickly, and it happened at two o'clock that same afternoon. They said the woman had gone crazy at her husband's sudden death. Any strange behavior was treated as madness.

Two days after the funeral, Helenice opened the restaurant early and was surprised by the appearance of Rosário, sitting in the doorway. The girl smiled and hugged her, babbling something in Cape Verdean Creole.

Helenice never understood how the girl had managed to find her way back home, how she was still alive, how she hadn't been run over, or kidnapped, or eaten by the dogs. Maybe it was African witchcraft.

"Who is stronger than God?! Who is stronger than God?!" she shouted, distressed, taking little Rosário by the arm, determined to rid herself of the child again before Madeinusa woke up.

CAPTIVITY

It was Wednesday when Madeinusa asked Adriano to take her urgently to Francisco's parents' house. She needed to talk to Samuel. She walked into Chico the Gravedigger's house without asking permission, interrupting their conversation.

"Is it true you hear a voice singing at five o'clock every morning?"

Samuel was in a daze.

"Since the day I arrived in the head, at five in the morning and five in the afternoon. Do you know the girl?" His eyes were alight with hope.

"What does she sing?" Madeinusa was nervous.

"Different songs each time. I've counted five of them."

"Five?" She became even more anxious. "What are the words? What do they say?"

"I don't really understand. It sounds like another language, but sometimes I can catch a few words."

"What words?"

"Farewell. Heart. Sea. Home."

"The *mornas*!" Madeinusa was crying. "Oh God!"

"What?"

"Rosário's *mornas*. I'm sure of it."

"Who's Rosário?" asked Samuel.

"My sister, on my father's side. She's African, her mother used to sing *mornas*, they're songs from there, from Cape Verde. Rosário used to do the same. Every day, at five in the morning and five in the afternoon, ever since she was little."

"And how do those songs end up in the saint's head?" asked Francisco.

"The *mornas* are a prayer to her mother," said Madeinusa.

"And do you know where she lives?" asked Francisco.

"No, she disappeared when my father died. The only other thing I want in life is to find Rosário. My mother said some relatives came to fetch her the day my father died, but I don't believe her. I've been dreaming about her and my father all these years, and that was how I knew she was my sister."

"How come?" asked Samuel.

"My father spoke to me in my dream. It was only when I was older that I understood that Mother hated Rosário because she was the child of my father's betrayal with another woman. I've been trying for years, done everything I could, but haven't been able to find a single clue. My mother can't know anything about this, right?"

"She knows already," said Francisco. "She heard it on the radio when Aécio announced Samuel was looking for the

Singing Voice. She came to ask me what he knew about 'that singing girl.'"

"And what did you say?"

"That he didn't know anything. But if it made Helenice so angry, we were certainly going to find out about her."

"You didn't even tell me about that conversation," Samuel complained.

"I've only just remembered; I didn't think it was important. The old woman hates music—I thought that was why she was so mad."

"She hates Rosário. I suspected terrible things; I thought Rosário was dead. Even mentioning Rosário's name was forbidden in our house." Madeinusa was silent for a moment. Then she asked: "And in the head, there's no way you can talk back to her, Samuel?"

"I can only listen."

"Maybe if Aécio keeps mentioning it on the radio she'll show up," said Francisco.

"It's our only chance. We don't even know where she lives, but if I can hear her in the head, she can't be too far away."

"I'll do anything I can to find her," said Madeinusa.

CELL

When Madeinusa left, the others resumed their conversation at the point they'd stopped: the great misfortune. Only someone who had lived through the year of Candeia's misfortune knew the real name of Meticuloso, the man who had ruined the townspeople's lives. Chico the Gravedigger had known him very well; they'd played together on the square as boys. They had lost touch when Manoel's work had started to take him out on the road to other towns.

When he returned to Candeia to work on constructing St. Anthony, Manoel had sought out his childhood friend to drink cachaça and lime and talk about life. His life was Mariinha. He had talked about her gentle hands, her innocence, the child she was expecting. He said how happy she was at his success with the building of the saint. The money he was making was more than enough to go and fetch Mariinha and their son. They could live with his mother for a bit while he built a house for them. This was before the engineer had gone away and the mistake had put an end to his life.

"Is he buried here?" asked Samuel.

"No. They say he hanged himself and was buried right there, in your grandmother Niceia's house. Nobody else has ever been inside. Practically the whole family fled. Those who remained went mad."

"You must leave here, child," Gerusa interrupted him, pleading. "If you've come to find your father, you know now that he's no longer with us."

"My friend Manoel was a good man, you can be sure of that. That head caused his misfortune and it's responsible for yours, too, I can see that now. Leave now before you end up dead like your father."

"But we're making money, the people are happy, there are weddings every day—where's the harm in that?" objected Francisco.

"That money is cursed. If that's where it's coming from, I'd rather go hungry."

Gerusa's words put a stop to Francisco's insistence.

Samuel couldn't think. It was already late, and the only thing he wanted at that point was to spend his last night in the head of the saint, listen to the Singing Voice by way of a farewell and then leave, forever. But it was dangerous to go back to the head, and Francisco was worried for his friend.

"Wait. It's risky, but I've got a plan that might help you," said Francisco to Samuel.

Francisco went ahead and unlocked the cemetery gate. There were still crowds of people there. They were crying, and at first Francisco and Samuel couldn't understand what the commotion was about.

"They said there's a truck of explosives on its way to Candeia," said one of the men. "Helenice went to Fortaleza to talk to Osório and he gave an order for the saint's head to be blown up."

There were about four hundred people in the crowd, with more arriving every minute, following the rumors of the planned explosion of St. Anthony's head.

The head was Samuel's misfortune, but even so he wanted to spend his last night there. This might be his last chance to hear the Singing Voice and the *mornas,* to fish for any clue as to where she might be. All he wanted to do was spend the night in the head.

Before five in the morning, the trucks of explosives arrived in Candeia. There were TV crews with them to film the spectacle, the end of the sacrilege against St. Anthony.

Helenice was with Osório, and she looked triumphant. Samuel was found by two of Osório's henchmen and taken to the old police station, which was reopened specially. He was thrown into a corner of a cell that was dark and filthy from years without use.

It was Osório who made the rules in Candeia, and they were brutal. Samuel knew that the henchmen had received explicit orders not to let anyone in. No visitors, not so much as a glass of water. The boy accused of being an imposter in Candeia, of disturbing public order, would remain in the cell until the explosives had been set up. Then he would be given a few hours to leave the town, to return only on pain of death. Osório would come back to live in Candeia to sort everything out, and all the people who had raided the abandoned houses would be kicked out. After the head, those old houses would also be demolished.

Osório had been determined in his plan. For years he had waited for the final inhabitants to quit Candeia. There were few remaining, very few. Helenice had already agreed to sell her house. Chico the Gravedigger's peace-loving family could be moved elsewhere, doubtless without too much resistance. The few older people still there would die soon. It was just a matter of time.

The plan was to sell the land of Candeia to a company that would build a factory there, but Osório couldn't do this until all the houses were in his name.

Samuel's gift had given new life to the town, a town that when completely dead could have made the ex-mayor's fortune. Helenice had always known about the plan, always supported it, for she wanted to leave that place. The offer on her house would be enough for her to go. Her past would be buried beneath a factory forever.

In prison, Samuel was getting more and more anxious with every passing minute. He had no idea what was happening. He heard cries on the road, people calling his name. Francisco's voice was the most desperate. Madeinusa, Adriano, all of them were there, outside. Osório and the engineers charged with carrying out the explosion were meeting in Helenice's house. Father Zacarias had tried to intercede, but in vain. He had not even been allowed to enter the prison. Samuel, however, after so many hours of hunger and solitude, could hardly believe his eyes when he saw his grandmother Niceia on the other side of the bars, looking in at her grandson with tender devotion.

PART FOUR

COUNSEL

"You're as strong as I am. You cannot deny that you are my grandson."

Samuel was hungry, thirsty, uneasy and could find no trace of strength in his condition. His feelings for the crazy old woman were confused. He was scared, he was angry, but it still mattered to him that she remained the only living link to his past. He smiled a little, trying to acknowledge her presence.

"How did you get in here?"

"You must fulfill the promises you made to your mother."

She annoyed him when she ignored his questions.

"I've done that already."

"Not everything."

"What's missing?" Samuel asked, though he did remember—he would never forget his mother's last words. He was only asking to test the old woman.

"The candles. You only lit the one for Father Cicero. There's still the one for St. Anthony, and another for St. Francis."

"I've carried out the most important request."

"You have. You came here to Candeia."

"I came just to suffer."

"You are brave. You bore it all. You were a real man."

"And I'm going to leave just the way I arrived: pushed out as if I were a filthy rat."

"That's not true."

"You don't know anything. I went hungry for sixteen days, I got sick, I had no one to give me shelter, and I got myself involved with this madness around the saint."

"Are you angry with the saint?"

"Very! I've always been angry with the saints and I'm even angrier now. They're only good for deceiving stupid people into parting with their money."

"Your mother thought differently."

"She was too good. She lived and died never seeing any malice in the world. Poor and wretched and buried in a hammock."

Samuel wept. He hated crying, but he cried in front of his grandmother, that decrepit old woman who, yet again, was unable to help.

"She asked you to light a candle for St. Anthony. You have to do so before you leave."

"I don't want anything to do with any saint now."

"Mariinha said she wanted the candles lit at the saints' feet. You'll have to climb the hill to light the one to St. Anthony."

"I'm locked up, so that will be easy," said Samuel with a note of sarcasm.

"You'll be released in a few hours."

"If I climb that hill, I'll get bitten again, and I'll get locked up again."

"The dogs are mine. They won't bite you. And you won't be locked up again if you say you're leaving. Go up, light your candle and say a prayer to the saint."

Samuel laughed contemptuously.

"Pray? Me? Lady, you really are crazy."

"Praying is saying what you feel."

"I feel hatred."

"Then that's what you should say. Shout it good and loud; don't leave out a thing when you're talking to the saint."

"I may have your blood, but I'm not as crazy as you yet. I'm not going to do that."

Niceia was upset and moved closer to the bars.

"You can't leave here without lighting the candle your mother asked you for."

In those last words her voice took on a serious tone, and she looked Samuel in the eye: this was an order. And Mariinha's requests were the only laws in force in Samuel's life. Apart from them, there was nothing left.

"They're going to release you tomorrow morning. They want to know what route you're going to take. Tell them you're going that way, you're going over the hill and on through Inhamuns. There will undoubtedly be people following you. Everyone already knows you're going to be thrown out of town, that's the only thing they're talking about on the radio now."

"And whose side are the people on?"

"On the side of St. Anthony's messenger. When you leave,

there will be crowds outside the police station. Your friend Francisco hasn't stopped fighting for you. But nobody has any power without the law on their side."

"Are they going to blow up the head?"

"It's all set. They're going to wait for you to leave."

"I don't want to see it."

"I don't think you should, either."

Samuel looked at Niceia with the numbness of a goodbye. She moved away, about to leave. He knew it was too late to ask about his father.

"Thank you," he said. "I'll light my mother's candle because she asked me to. I don't know what will become of my life after I've crossed that hill. So, goodbye, then."

"Don't forget to pray. I'm asking that of you. Mariinha would ask you, if she were here. Farewell, Samuel, I hope you will be very happy."

CONFRONTATION

It was the first time Samuel had seen Osório. Up to that point he had only met his henchmen and heard of his reputation as a crook. The mayor came into the police station accompanied by Helenice and Father Zacarias. One of the henchmen opened the door to Samuel's cell and ordered him to remain seated. He needn't have bothered: Samuel barely had the strength to open his eyes. Helenice started firing off insults straightaway: "I don't know where the hell you've come from, but you're headed back there now. Nothing worthwhile can ever come from bad people. Just when we thought we were free of the misfortune, Meticuloso's son shows up to bring it back all over again."

Samuel said nothing. He wanted to speak, but Father Zacarias put his index finger to his lips, gesturing for Samuel to keep to himself whatever he had been thinking of saying.

"My child, I've been talking to Helenice and Osório and

asked them to give you a chance. The head is going to be blown up at five o'clock tomorrow afternoon, and they want you to be out by then."

"And never come back," said the woman with loathing. "The blood of the Vale family is tainted with the Devil's ink."

Osório was also glaring at Samuel, hatred in his eyes. The priest asked him something quietly; the mayor said yes grudgingly. Zacarias went over to the door and returned with Dr. Adriano, to examine Samuel, and Madeinusa, who had brought him milk, coconut water and a chicken broth.

While Dr. Adriano checked Samuel's pressure and heart rate, Madeinusa fed him, holding the straw of the glass of milk close to his mouth. He looked down at his belly. It was not clinging to his ribs.

"She's another one who inherited bad blood from her father," said Helenice, receiving a look of contempt from her own daughter.

This time it was Adriano who asked everyone to keep calm.

Samuel quickly recovered, and got up to leave and keep to the plan. There were indeed a lot of people outside the police station. The faithful, his friends, TV broadcasters, reporters, a sea of people dressed in brown.

An emotional Francisco ran forward to hug his friend. He recalled the day he'd seen him for the first time. By now the whole town knew of Osório's orders; the explosives were in place, and no one was allowed to get close to the head of the saint anymore.

With each step he took, Samuel was getting stronger. They walked, all of them, toward the house of Chico the Gravedigger: that would be the place from which he would set off, leaving town once and for all.

"Before I leave, I need to go to the saint's feet to light a candle."

Francisco thought this was funny.

"To St. Anthony?"

"I was asked to do it."

"You sure you can make it up there?" asked Madeinusa.

"I've got to. I can't leave Candeia without doing this."

"I've got a candle and matches," said Chico the Gravedigger.

"We'll go with you," said Adriano.

They stopped awhile to eat, have a bath, rest. Setting off to the top of the hill would be less obvious from there. Having woken up and eaten a good lunch of bean stew with curd cheese and cashew-fruit juice, Samuel felt ready for the climb. The walk would take a little over half an hour.

Adriano, Madeinusa and Chico the Gravedigger went with him, round the back of the hill so as not to attract the attention of the town's inhabitants—who fortunately were all gathered in front of the saint's head.

The closer they got to the decapitated body, the weirder the whole thing seemed. Down there was Candeia. The people looked like ants surrounding St. Anthony's head.

The pack of dogs that guarded the saint's body appeared.

There were more than ten of them, and they were nice and calm. They looked at Samuel as though he was someone they knew, without barking, without threats. The dog that had bitten him approached, wagging its tail. He recognized it from the marking on its forehead, the smudge in the fur that looked like a deformed star.

Chico the Gravedigger handed Samuel the box of matches and the candle. Now the dogs got nervous, barking as though they wanted to say something, walking toward the saint's feet. Samuel remembered that the candle had to be lit at the feet. He remembered Niceia asking him to express his anger about everything to the saint, and asked his friends to move back down the hill a little to allow him to pray for the first and last time in his life.

"I don't know how to pray, Mr. Saint. All I know is that up till now my life has been nothing but misfortune and it's your fault. You see all that, all that happening down there? You see these marks on my arm, from being scratched, from being punched? All your fault."

The candle wouldn't stay alight in the wind. As he tried to find some way to get it to burn so that he could leave, he kept talking: "I have no faith at all, old man. Even the candle I'm lighting isn't strong enough to keep its flame. This business of faith is what ruins poor people like me. I did actually believe, at first. When I saw those people getting married, I did believe in the miracle. Damned miracle."

Samuel started shouting. The dogs took fright.

"Damned miracle! There's no saint, there's no miracle."

Adriano wanted to go over to him, but Madeinusa prevented him. "Let the poor thing get it off his chest."

Samuel had anger in his voice, in his body, in his movements, in his feet as they kicked the enormous unfinished statue of St. Anthony.

"And this bloody candle still won't stay alight. Damned candle, damned saint, who ruined my life and my mother's life, too. The poor thing, she died still believing. You ruined the people of Candeia. Just look at this town. It's your fault. I hate this whole lie about St. Anthony. Hate it! I never want to see another saint in my life. Next time I see a saint's statue I'm going to smash it, I'm going to demolish it."

Samuel was getting more upset every minute. The dogs, which till that point had been lying on the ground around him, jumped to their feet. Some barked at Adriano, Madeinusa and Chico the Gravedigger, who were farther off now, nearly halfway down the hill.

"I never meant to hurt you."

The voice was coming from the feet of the saint.

"Who said that?"

Samuel was scared. He yelled again: "Who said that?"

"I never meant to hurt you, nor your mother, nor anybody in Candeia," answered the voice that came from the saint's feet.

"I've gone mad. Oh, Mother, I've gone mad! I don't want to hear any more voices." Samuel knelt on the ground, hands over his ears.

"For the love of God, forgive me! I so badly need to ask you for forgiveness, Samuel."

"How do you know my name, damned saint?"

"Because of the love I feel toward you."

Samuel had never imagined anything so scary could happen to him. After getting access to the women's prayers, now he could hear the voice of the saint? Coming from the toes of his decapitated body? He was going crazy, he was sure of it. All of a sudden the fear passed. Yes, he had been afraid at first, not knowing where that voice was coming from. But now he believed it could be the saint's voice. Only crazy people talk to saints. That being so, he thought, let's talk.

"That's just perfect. So the famous St. Anthony talks out of his feet?"

"I need to hear you say you'll forgive me."

"I thought it worked the other way round, that sinners asked saints for forgiveness. My poor mother, she died believing that."

"Mariinha was a saintly woman."

"And she died like an animal, scrawny, deep inside the hammock, thinking you or some other saint was going to turn up and save her from her wretchedness."

Samuel was almost crying. He remembered how he had only been happy when he was living beside his mother. He saw the road on which he had arrived, and along which he would be leaving. From the top of the hill he could see the statue of St. Francis in Canindé. "It serves you right that they're going to blow up that head. I hope they blow up this body, too. A saint who talks out of his feet doesn't deserve a statue."

"Are they going to blow up the body?"

"Aren't you supposed to know everything?"

"Did they say they're going to blow up the body? What's going to happen to me?"

The dogs had become very agitated. They approached the saint's left foot, barking loudly. Samuel went with them. There was forest all around, and they barked and barked, and the voice kept on talking, getting louder and louder, closer and closer. With the barking of the dogs it was impossible to hear what it was saying.

Madeinusa, Adriano and Chico the Gravedigger walked back up to the top of the hill to find out what was happening. The barking dogs were facing away from them and didn't see them approach. Samuel was in a cold sweat, pale. Dr. Adriano was concerned.

"You mustn't put yourself under this stress. We should go back down."

"Can you all hear the voice, too?" asked Samuel.

"Let's get out of here." Madeinusa was afraid.

The bushes next to the saint's foot moved suddenly, pushed aside by a human foot with long toenails that emerged from a hole in the statue. The diameter of the hole was just right for a very thin man to get through, and one did—in a pair of old trousers tied at the waist with an electric cable that served as a belt.

He looked confused, and covered his eyes with his hands to protect himself from the glare. The dogs gathered round him, no longer barking now. He was their master.

Samuel, Adriano and Madeinusa were afraid and drew

back. Chico the Gravedigger did the opposite. He came closer, gradually, till the man moved his hands from his face and he was able to be sure of what he'd suspected.

"Samuel, it's your father! It's your father, Manoel Meticuloso!"

CADAVER

Chico the Gravedigger hugged Manoel, but Samuel held back. He didn't recognize this man as his father. It wasn't a reunion—there was no question of love, no feeling of missing him to appease. His sixteen days' walking was intended to bring him to Candeia to kill this man who was standing in front of him, who gave his mother a child. Manoel, Meticuloso, who was responsible for the curse upon Candeia. The wheel had come full circle: Samuel had found his father. He gave up his initial plan straightaway—you don't kill someone who has already been so abandoned by life. Perhaps Manoel had only remained barely alive thanks to an intervention by the saint. Not that Samuel was now a man of faith, but he couldn't deny that St. Anthony had certain tricks up his sleeve.

While Adriano nervously sat the man down on the floor to examine him, Samuel went over to the hole out of which his father had appeared a few seconds earlier. He was the same height and almost the same weight, so he was able to get through it to the inside of the statue.

It was clear that the body of the saint was Manoel's house, and had been for many years. He'd used his skill in design and building work to make the hollow body, open at the neck, into a spacious home, with conditions that were basic but comfortable.

In the corner Samuel could see a stash of bits of wood, bottles of water, pieces of cloth, old clothes—material used to make this home's furniture. Manoel had an old mattress as his bed; it was covered with a bedspread, tidily made. A stove, still smoking, was topped by an old pan with watery soup made of who knew what. Apart from its grotesque location, the house was well set up. All organized, everything in its little place. It seemed Manoel must creep out of his hiding place in search of rubbish, for the results of his foraging could be seen in his furniture, in the blankets made up of old scraps. Perhaps the cold night wind drove Manoel under those improvised covers. Perhaps from there, by the saint's feet, he could see the moon. Alone, for years, in this strange house inside a saint.

The hollow body was well ventilated and suffocating at the same time. More beautiful and frightening—much more—than the head of the saint. This is my father's house, Samuel thought. This is where he has lived all this time.

It was lovely looking up and seeing the clouds go by, peacefully, through the hole in the neck. Samuel felt a sense of calm as he watched them, distracting himself by trying to guess at their shapes. They kept moving, in slow motion, without the slightest interest in what was happening down below.

Adriano called out to Samuel, who hurried out of the body.

From up high on the hill they could see that Osório had brought in reinforcements from the neighboring police forces, and judging by the movement of men approaching and entering one house after another, Samuel guessed they were looking for him. Did Helenice and Osório know that he hadn't yet left, that he hadn't taken the chance that they'd given him to leave right away?

Samuel understood that he couldn't fight against Osório's dangerous weapons; he wouldn't be able to avoid an agonizing spell in prison. He had found his father. Now he had to run away.

They went back down the hill as quickly as they could, carrying Manoel Meticuloso, who didn't take his eyes off his son. The man's appearance was frightening. A beard grown over many years, yellowish, sunken cheeks, thin, decrepit body, with hardly any resemblance to a human being, almost as much an animal as were his dogs.

"Let's go straight to our place," said Chico.

Manoel disagreed.

"I want to go to my mother's house."

"Maybe it'd be safer," said Samuel. "No one dares go in there."

"I don't either," said Madeinusa. "No way am I setting foot in that place."

“I’m staying with her.” Adriano was losing his nerve, too.

“We three can go, Samuel.” Chico the Gravedigger was hardly afraid of anything.

During the descent they could see that almost the whole town was standing around the head, waiting for the explosion, which was the only reason the three of them were able to get to Niceia’s house without being noticed.

Perhaps they all imagined the house would be filthy, dark, rat-infested, overgrown by the forest, but they were surprised to find a living room that was tidy and clean, as though the flow of life here had never stopped.

At last Samuel was going into his grandmother’s house, and this time it wasn’t sealed up. As though she was expecting them, the gate was open, no chain, just like all the gates and doors on the abandoned houses. And Samuel’s grandmother was not at home. He called out to her, to no avail. In the first bedroom they came to, there was a red crocheted bedspread covering the single bed, on which they placed Manoel. Chico told Samuel to stay with his father while he went to find some water.

The old man motioned for his son to sit down on a stool next to the bed.

“What I wanted to do was go back to your mother. . . .”

“Chico told me. I know the whole story.”

“Did your mother forgive me?”

“Before she died she asked me to come and find you. You never went there, not even for a visit.”

“I couldn’t. I was so ashamed after I’d ruined the lives of all these people. My life fell apart. But you came to save the town?”

"What do you mean, save it? All I did was deceive these people."

"I know you really could hear them."

"How do you know?"

"Everything you said in the head I could hear in the body. At first I didn't know who you were, but my mother came to tell me."

Chico the Gravedigger and his wife returned with water and food and interrupted the conversation. Francisco stayed outside the house, having lost his nerve since the cameraman's experience, but he asked for his friend to come out and talk to him at the gate.

"They've delayed the explosion till tomorrow."

"Why?"

"Apparently there's some TV crew coming from Rio de Janeiro. They decided to wait."

"I don't want to see it," said Samuel.

"And you can't. The law is looking for you, you've got to run. They've made up all kinds of things—they say we stole money from all those ignorant people. I tried to say it was all my fault, but no one believes me," explained Francisco.

"You lie so often there's no longer any point trying to be honest."

They both laughed.

"There's something else. The whole town somehow already knows Meticuloso was living in the body of the saint. Soon the authorities will be looking for him, too."

Francisco passed on a hug and a message from Madeinusa: there was no sign of Rosário. But she wouldn't give up on the search and hoped that one day she'd find her. Now, without any access to the head, she had lost the only clue to her sister's whereabouts. It might be impossible, but she would try.

Samuel nodded, glad someone would continue his search. He looked over at the town. All he could see were bright spotlights illuminating the head in anticipation of the explosion.

"It's like a horror film."

"What's the old lady's house like inside?"

"Normal. Nice and tidy."

"Really? I never would have thought it!"

They heard the sound of people approaching. Francisco started to hurry.

"Aécio told me to tell you that he'll come here at four in the morning to take you away. He's got hold of a hat, glasses, even a wig."

"I'll spend the night here, it's safest."

"Oh, it couldn't be safer. Even I don't dare go in."

An infinite silence, that in reality lasted just fractions of a second, made them realize that what they were experiencing was a goodbye. Samuel was confused and tired, and in a few hours he would no longer have the company of Francisco, the most loyal and faithful friend he would ever meet.

A police car drove past Niceia's house. Samuel ducked so as not to be seen. Francisco walked along the pavement and crossed the road.

Back inside the house, Manoel and Chico didn't stop talking and crying as night drew in. Even though Samuel needed to sleep, even though he could hardly bear the tiredness of that difficult day, he gave in to his curiosity and walked all around Niceia's house with a candle in his hand.

Nothing different or unusual to see. Nothing to justify the desperate terror of the cameraman, who had never told anyone what he'd witnessed inside. He went along the corridor, through the kitchen, the yard, the bedrooms, the living room, the bathrooms. All tidy, a living house, with water in the taps, no dust on the furniture.

Samuel came into his father's bedroom to say goodbye to him and to Chico the Gravedigger.

Manoel was asleep. Samuel could only give him a glance, no more than that. He looked at the fragile figure of the man who had been living inside a hollow body all the time Samuel was growing up, all the time Mariinha was dying.

Chico the Gravedigger got up to give Samuel the hug he needed. They thanked each other for everything. Chico said Dr. Adriano had promised to take care of his father until he was restored to normal strength. Dr. Adriano didn't know how he had survived, actually. His body bore signs of snakebites, malnutrition, skin diseases and possibly lung damage, too.

Chico the Gravedigger tried to convince Samuel to think about another way out.

"If you stay, here in this house, maybe no one will come in. Everyone's scared. We'll even help to spread more rumors about ghosts, just until the mayor gives up."

"It's not as easy as that, Chico—he's not going to give up, not ever. What he wants is to get rid of everyone and sell Candeia."

"And Rosário?"

"What about her?"

"Don't you want to find Rosário?"

"The head's filled with explosives. How am I supposed to go in there to hear any news of her? It's over, Chico. I wasn't born to have a happy ending."

"The ending—the real ending, Samuel—doesn't come till I lower your coffin into the grave. There's still time."

"You're a real dreamer, Chico."

"I learned that from death. The time to dream is when you're still aboveground."

Just then, Manoel awoke babbling, crying from his pain. A pain that he called Mariinha. Chico brought a glass of water to the man's mouth, but he choked, then turned purple, and then he calmed down and went back to sleep. After that, Chico the Gravedigger left.

Samuel set up a green hammock beside his father's bed. He chatted to him, talked about this and that in his life, suspecting his father wasn't following any of it. They fell asleep at last, defeated by their fatigue.

Through the early hours Samuel awoke several times, sure that he'd heard the voice of his grandmother, who still hadn't appeared since Manoel's return. Each time he looked, he found no one in the house. He looked in the living room, in the kitchen, in all the bedrooms.

Almost all. The fifth time he woke, he investigated the house yet again and noticed that on the left-hand side there was a locked door. At first he thought it must be a cupboard for storing bits and pieces, but then he felt a need to open it. He had to force the door, but once it was open he found a bedroom containing a large double bed covered in a black crocheted bedspread with a tulle mosquito net over the top.

As he came as close as he could, he saw the mummified body of an elderly woman, in the dress Niceia had been wearing every time she had met him. This woman—it was Niceia herself—had been dead for many years. Her sparse white hair was spread over her skull, which was covered in dry, skinlike strips of dried beef. Her hands, clasped together, held a Mother of God rosary that hypnotized Samuel: amid the blue beads, he could see the one green bead from the rosary that had belonged to Mariinha.

Faced with the dead body of his grandmother, he wept at the misfortune of his crooked fate. It was true that life hadn't given him very many chances to dream, but he did stubbornly insist on it. He had wanted to leave Juazeiro and carry on to the sea. He'd wanted to see that massive expanse of water and swim out against the waves. He'd always thought of Candeia as a quick stop on the way to his final destination.

A few hours from now he would be leaving, and he might be able to make it to the beach the same day. He had money. Francisco could visit him in Fortaleza, bring him news of his father. Or Francisco could come and live with him, if Candeia really was destroyed by the sale of the tiny town's land.

"I knew the girl."

It was Niceia's voice.

"Looked just like her father, even when she was little. I don't know how she managed to stay alive."

"Where is she?"

"That I don't know. I never saw her again."

"You're lying. You knew about my father."

Niceia raised herself up from the bed, walked past Samuel and out toward Manoel's room and, with her back still turned, said: "You should go soon, the rain's coming."

"But the sky is clear."

"That young man is here already. May God keep you."

Niceia was right. It was nearly four o'clock and Aécio was at his post, sitting in his car with the engine running, waiting to take Samuel away from Candeia. There was only time for Samuel to pick up a candle and a box of matches before walking out of that house, getting into the car and leaving.

CANINDÉ

"I need to stop in Canindé before I leave."

"Why?"

"I promised my mother I'd light a candle at the feet of St. Francis. Her soul is not yet at peace. I made a promise."

"I'll only take you because I'm afraid of spirits, with all due respect to your late mother. But it's a dangerous thing to do."

"I know."

"So put on your disguise. On the backseat there's a coat, a wig, a hat and mustache. And in the coat pocket Madeinusa left you a notebook with everyone's phone numbers: mine, hers, the doctor's, the radio station's. She asked you to call every couple of days for news of Rosário. We'll find the girl, the poor thing, I believe that. Adriano is going from house to house making enquiries. You never heard anything else?"

"Never."

"What scares me is that Helenice might have done something really foolish."

"Me too."

They only had to go two streets before they hit the tarmac and were on their way out of Candeia, so there was no time for nostalgic thoughts, for saying goodbye to everyone or going to the head one last time. Samuel wasn't just going on some journey, he was running away.

The car drove past Dona Rosa's house. The two chairs stood outside, in the same place as on the first day, empty. Perhaps the owners had upheld the tradition of dying in their beds inside the house. The cat was alive, on top of the wall. It looked up at the noise of the car but went back to sleep.

"What was it like, finding your father?" Aécio broke the silence.

"Strange. I thought the saint was talking to me."

"All those years in that body and nobody knew a thing. How awful."

"He had some little hiding places in there, underground. He had his dogs, he had his mother. He was protected, waiting for death."

"You don't want to stay with him?"

"No, he has people with him. I've done what I needed to do."

Samuel seemed to be finding the conversation uncomfortable, and Aécio decided to turn on the car radio, tuning in to his own station. The daily *Roberto Carlos Special* was starting. It was a taped recording, always the same sequence of Roberto Carlos songs, but the station had never received a single complaint about the show that played the classics of the man they called the King.

"Do you like the King's music?"

"I do. My mother used to love him."

They listened to the first song in silence, soaking in the lyrics that talked of a strange power, until the chorus, when Aécio joined in at the top of his voice, making Samuel laugh.

"What? It's Roberto Carlos's best song, kid!"

"You're the one I'm laughing at, idiot. And it's not Roberto Carlos's song either, this one; he just sings it."

"Course it is!"

"No, the words were written by Caetano Veloso. Someone gave my mother the record, and she used to take it over to play on our neighbor Radiola's gramophone when I was little. I read the record sleeve, it said it right there: Caetano Veloso. He's completely different from Roberto Carlos. I've seen him on TV."

"But it's the King who sings it, that's the important thing."

"Either way, I never really understood it."

"What?"

"This business about a strange power. Do you know what that is?"

"What what is? The strange power?"

"Yes."

"Do I know? Well, I do, but I just can't explain it."

"That's no help."

"It's like something you know when you see it. The strange power appears and—bam!—you feel it. When it's taken hold of us we do what we have to do whatever the cost, and wild horses won't hold us back. I think it comes from God."

"That's what my mother thought, too. I asked her."

"And have you ever felt it, that strange power, about anything?"

"Yes, I've felt it a lot."

"And what do you think?"

"At first it used to come from my mother. After she died, it stopped. But sometimes inside the head I used to feel it, too."

"Because of the saint?"

"No, because of Rosário's voice."

COURAGE

A few Roberto Carlos songs later, they reached Canindé. Aécio's plan had been to give Samuel the money from Francisco and then drive him somewhere, but Samuel said he'd stay here.

"Be really careful, man. Osório is saying you've got money with you that you stole from the poor. They're going to try and get you."

"Yes, but I'm not going to be taking the money. You can give it back."

"And how are you going to live?"

"As I have done before. Broke, wretched, hopeless. I'll hitch a lift today—I know how to take care of myself. I want to see the sea."

"Just be careful, then. Call me if you need anything. If you end up staying in Canindé, let me know."

Samuel hugged his friend, hurrying their goodbye. Then

he turned his back and started to walk up the steps that led to St. Francis. There was nobody around, no danger. The problem was, Mariinha wanted the candle lit at the saint's feet, and there was a reflecting pool around St. Francis. Samuel would have to cross it without soaking the matches, the candle and the notebook of phone numbers.

"It's shallow, you can walk across. But it stinks."

A ten-year-old boy was sitting on the floor, watching Samuel.

"If it gets wet I've got another candle I can sell you."

"I've not got any money, kid—scram."

"I'll scram when I want to."

Samuel ignored him. He took off his coat, his shirt and shoes. He piled them up tidily on the floor with his notebook. He put the candles and matches in his hat and walked into the water with his hands above his head. He crossed the water without any trouble and was soon at the feet of the saint.

"Right then, Mother. I've lit your third candle. I've kept my promise. I went to Candeia, found my grandmother dead, found my father and now I'm leaving. Your blessing, Mother. From now on, it's all down to me."

From that height Samuel could catch a glimpse of the CE-020 bus. He was planning to walk down and try to get a ride on it to Fortaleza. Returning through the reflecting pool was a little easier with his hat on his head, but there was a problem: the boy had stolen his clothes. He was standing there, in the distance, holding it all in his hands and laughing at Samuel. The biggest problem was the notebook of telephone numbers—his only link to his friends in Candeia, his only hope of getting news of Rosário, if she was still alive.

The boy ran down a small gully on the saint's left-hand side, and Samuel went after him, barefoot and soaked. The mustache, hat and wig fell by the wayside. This little brat was quick—soon he'd darted into a road of houses, one after another, before stopping and looking back, waiting for Samuel.

"There's no money there, kid, it's just old clothes and paper," said Samuel, panting.

"I know. I'm not after money."

"Take whatever you want, then, just leave the notebook on the ground. I'll go away, I won't tell anyone."

"I don't want any of it. Only, my grandfather wants to talk to you."

"Who's your grandfather?"

"My mum's dad."

"Where is he?"

"On the Rua das Graças. Come on, I'll show you."

The two of them walked a bit farther, up to a house with a door and window opening onto the street. Samuel followed the boy inside and saw a woman he recognized but had no idea where from.

"Did you bring him?" asked a man's voice.

"He's here, in the living room, completely covered in mud," the boy called out.

The man came in to talk to Samuel. He, too, looked familiar.

"Remember me?"

"I do, but I don't know where from."

"Must be because of my clothes."

He smiled at Samuel. Only gradually did Samuel come to recognize in that kindly-looking man the pilgrim who had helped him on the road before he arrived in Candeia.

"Do you want a change of clothes? Yours are filthy."

"No need."

"Chica, bring the boy a change of clothes."

Theirs was a small house, and very humble. The wall facing the door was covered in pictures of saints. Side by side were Father Cicero, St. Anthony and St. Francis, the holy trinity of Samuel's recent days.

The woman brought him clothes. It was the same woman who had been on the road the day he'd met that man. She was friendly now.

"You helped my sister get married, young man. Thank you for that."

"You're welcome. How did you know?"

She excused herself, but before leaving the living room she looked at her husband, as though that were a code for something that was about to happen. She hurried back with a plate of *cuscuz,* then brought milk and a cup of coffee. With her feet she pushed a tall stool toward Samuel, put down the food and quickly went out into the yard.

"Look, mister . . ."

"Francisco José."

"Well, Mr. Francisco José, I appreciate your kindness, but I don't understand anything. What is it you want from me?"

"I'm a friend, and I've got something to tell you. Something you need to know before you leave. It's about Rosário."

"How do you know about that?"

"I'm Madeinusa's uncle, Helenice's brother. But she doesn't consider me her brother because I'm her father's son with the housemaid. She's forgotten I exist, and that's what rescues the whole story."

"How so?"

"When Fernando came back from Cape Verde with Rosário, he told me the truth, a secret from Helenice. I knew she might try something with the girl."

"And did she?"

"She did. And I was the one who brought her back home when she was abandoned on the road. Everyone thought St. Francis had performed a miracle."

Samuel was frightened by the man's tone, which grew ever more emotional.

"Then Helenice locked the girl up in a house, but I never stopped having dreams where Fernando told me to go and rescue her. So I went. I found Rosário and got her out of that terrible place. Helenice doesn't know, she never found out. Nor did Madeinusa. Rosário is terrified of being killed like her father. We all are."

"Do you know where she lives?"

"In the little house out the back."

Samuel was completely stunned, wanting to hear more, wanting to run out to the backyard.

"This whole time? She's never been out?"

"Only to go to school. But she did go to Candeia once, in disguise."

"When?"

"To Madeinusa's wedding. She saw you there, but we left very quickly."

"And she's really here? Just out the back?"

"She is. She knows you're looking for her. She heard it on the radio. Aécio said you'd be at the foot of the saint; that's why I sent the kid to fetch you. Sorry about him stealing your clothes; that wasn't part of the plan."

"Can I talk to her?"

"That's why I sent him to bring you here."

Between Francisco José's home and the little house out the back there was a small yard. Samuel heard the *morna,* the same song he used to hear inside the head of the saint. Rosário sensed his presence and came out of the house shyly. She sat down on a crooked wooden bench outside her little room. Samuel sat beside her and waited for her to finish her song before saying his first words: "Thank you."

"What for?"

"For your songs. I heard them every day."

"I didn't know that until recently. But I dreamed about you."

"About me?"

"I did. Ever since I was a little girl I've dreamed about things that were going to happen. My mother's death, my father's, the man dressed in a St. Francis tunic coming to save me. All that I saw first in my dreams."

"Are you sure it was me?"

"I'm sure."

"And what was it like, your dream?"

"Strange. And brief. You were there, on your knees, lighting three candles. And there was a voice that took me a while to understand."

"A man's voice or a woman's?"

"A man's."

"What was he saying?"

"'Courage,' 'forgiveness,' 'love,' one word for each candle. 'Courage,' 'forgiveness,' 'love.' Do you understand it?"

He took the girl's hand in his and felt that strange power. Mariinha's candles, the course that led to Rosário. He wanted to take her to see the sea, to listen to her *mornas* forever, and for the first time things were beginning to make sense. He thought about the head of the saint, about Manoel's misfortune.

"Yes, I think I understand."

"Tell me, then: what does the dream mean?"

"You are my miracle, Rosário. That's what it means."

ACKNOWLEDGMENTS

My original ideas for this novel were written in 2006 for the "How to Tell a Story" screenwriting workshop led by Gabriel García Márquez at the Escuela de Cine y TV at San Antonio de los Baños, in Cuba, between the second and fifth of December.

The praise, enthusiasm and encouragement I received from García Márquez around this project were fundamental to its completion, and so I begin my thanks with him. More than that: this book is for him. I am also grateful to EICTV, to María Julia and to Alquimia, for the chance to be part of the final group to participate in this prestigious workshop.

Many thanks to Paulo Linhares, Bete Jaguaribe and Orlando Senna and to the Ministry of Culture's Programme for Cultural Dissemination and Exchange. To my highly experienced and talented coursemates: Ana Maria Parra (Colombia), Juan Pablo Bustamante (Colombia), Ernesto Villalobos (Costa Rica), Lien Lau (Cuba), Karina Narpier (Dominican Republic), Joaquín Guerrero Casasola (Mexico), Christian Ayala Alonso (Spain), Rocío Santillana (Peru) and our teacher, Fernando León de Aranoa.

I would also like to thank my friends Luciana Cruz, Mariana Cordiviolla, Janaína Marques, Marcus Moura, Rita Célia

Faheina, Manoella Monteiro, Samuel Macedo, Fátima Souza, Sheila Jacob, Silvia Jacob, Lira Neto, Lula Buarque de Holanda, Letícia Monte, Lilian Contreira, Regina Ribeiro, Fernanda Coutinho, Luciana Gifoni, Frei Betto, Natália Guerellus and Joana Medrado, the teachers Robert McKee and Guillermo Arriaga, Ary Leite, Thelma Leite, Cintia Figueiredo, Tiago Coutinho, Luciana Limaverde, Nícia Barroso, João Daniel Almeida, Paloma Jorge Amado, Cecília Amado, Ana Márcia Diógenes, Rosângela Primo, the Alencar family, the Acioli family, Sarah Odedina and Isabel Lopes Coelho.

I am grateful to professors Lívia Reis (my supervisor), Eurídice Figueiredo and Victor Hugo, who assessed this work for the qualifying exam for the Doctorate in Literary Studies at Universidade Federal Fluminense, shining the necessary light on it to develop the novel and bring it to the next stage.

To Dauna Vale, who took me to visit the real head of the saint, in Caridade.

To Neda Blythman and João Marcelo Melo, for their welcome in Cape Verde.

To the careful and incisive reading from my dear friend Julia Bussius, my editor at Companhia das Letras, whose work was crucial for this book.

To Diana Passy, Nathália Dimambro and Clara Dias, for the warm welcome in their new home.

To the voice of Mayra Andrade, whose music was the sound track to the writing of this book.

To my dear agent and friend, Lucia Riff, for all her support and encouragement.

And to José Marcos and Beatriz, my family, for this love that we share, which grows every day.

ABOUT THE TRANSLATOR

Daniel Hahn is a British writer, editor, and translator. He is the author of a number of works of nonfiction, including the history book *The Tower Menagerie,* and is one of the editors of *The Ultimate Book Guide,* a series of reading guides for children and teenagers, the first volume of which won the Blue Peter Book Award.

His translation of *The Book of Chameleons* by José Eduardo Agualusa won the Independent Foreign Fiction Prize. A former chair of the Translators Association, he is the national program director of the British Centre for Literary Translation and a trustee of the free expression charity English PEN.

ABOUT THE AUTHOR

Socorro Acioli was born in Fortaleza, Ceará, Brazil. She is a journalist and has a master's degree in Brazilian literature and a PhD in literary studies. She started her writing career in 2001 and since then has published books in various genres, including children's short stories and YA novels, and has received Brazil's most prestigious prize for children's literature, the Jabuti Prize.

In 2006, she was selected to take part in a workshop conducted by Nobel Prize winner Gabriel García Márquez. The author was selected by García Márquez himself based on her synopsis for *The Head of the Saint*. In 2007, she was a visiting researcher at a university in Germany, and she has lectured in several other countries, including Portugal, Bolivia, and Cape Verde. Acioli is also a translator, essayist, and literary theory teacher.